HOME RUN

The second pitch was faster with a bit of a curve on it. But now John's eye was ready for the pace and movement of the baseball. The bat swung and the ball sailed away, over the head of the boy playing out in right field . . .

'Every bat and every ball has what we call a "sweet spot",' said Rick, patting John on the back. 'Guess you got the sweet spot that time.'

Laurence and Matthew James

Home Run

A Magnet Book

This is for Julia who proves that silence can, indeed, be golden, but words can certainly be silver. With our thanks and appreciation.

First published as a Magnet paperback original 1988
by Methuen Children's Books Ltd
11 New Fetter Lane, London EC4P 4EE
Copyright © 1988 Laurence James
Printed and bound in Great Britain by
Cox & Wyman Ltd, Reading

ISBN 0 416 11882 8

John Greene paused for a moment, fighting for breath. He leant against the rough brick of the high warehouse wall, listening to the sound of the pursuing feet drawing closer, the sound beating and echoing through the maze of narrow alleys and courtyards all about him. John's heart was racing and every breath felt as if it was being drawn across hot sandpaper. He glanced around, trying to check his bearings, working out which way had the best chance of a clean escape.

The pursuit was closing on him. John looked at his watch, angling the face to catch the last crimson glow of the setting sun. It was just after nine o'clock on a warm July evening. The boy could feel sweat running down his back, inside the dark blue T-shirt, chilling him.

It was just his luck. There'd been six of them, and they'd split up, scattering in all directions. And John was the only one being chased.

The building at his side was the old storage warehouse for Chambers and Winston, 'Purveyors of Malt Vinegar to Persons of Taste', as the almost illegible, faded blue letters said, high above his head. At the far end was Inkerman Alley, cutting through past Alexander Terrace. From there, he'd have a choice of

5

going for Camden High Road with its crowds and its buses, or he could run for Primrose Hill and hide up somewhere around the goods depot. Both routes would take him in the general direction of home, to the west of the Caledonian Road, close by Holloway.

From the sound, the man pursuing him had stopped, probably listening for the noise of John's Adidas trainers slapping on the worn cobbles. The boy tried to still his own breathing, fighting for control. It had already been a long hard run. At school he was one of the top sprinters, but anything over eight hundred metres left him panting.

Still trying to decide which way to go, the tall teenager began to step quietly along the windowless wall, past several narrow side courts and alleys, dating back to Victorian times. He'd already been later than he should have been in heading for home, which was going to mean a heavy scene with his stepfather when he eventually made it back.

The shadows were deepening, the wedges of blackness slicing out across his path. John was looking down again at his watch when the hand came out of the darkness and grabbed him by the shoulder.

'Got you now, you . . . !'

John dropped suddenly into a crouch, pulling himself clear of the gripping fingers. He dived to his left and sprinted desperately towards Alexander Terrace. The angry yell drifted away behind him as he ran, arms pumping, head back. A ragged sheet of gleaming black plastic floated in front of him and he hurdled it like Ed Moses in his prime, turning left along the road, past a couple of gaping housewives. Now the noise of pounding feet was behind him again and he heard a yell for someone to stop him.

A skinny man, with thinning hair, carrying a handful of oily tools, came out of a front door, mouth opening as the boy dashed along the pavement. If he could reach the High Road there was always a bus to hop aboard. Always. It was only a couple of hundred metres further.

'Stop him!'

The woman who stepped out from the other side of the road was wearing the distinctive uniform of a traffic warden, holding her hand up in front of John as though he were a runaway double-decker.

He could have dodged around her, but he knew it would slow him down. And he was running out of breath again.

John ducked into the side-turning that was bounded by the little kids' playground and the abandoned slaughterhouse; a gloomy cavern that used to scare him rigid when he was younger, with rusting hooks dangling from ponderous girders and troughs stained with what older boys swore was clotted blood.

It suddenly seemed much darker, and much colder, with the towering walls of dusty red brick closing out the last shreds of the failing sun. John remembered that this particular alley led out on to a flat, open piece of land with the childrens' playground at its centre. There was a stitch biting in under his ribs, feeling like there was a ferret nibbling at his stomach, and he

7

knew that he couldn't run much further. And if he left the passageway there'd be nowhere to hide.

An opening beckoned on his right and he dived into it, sprinting into the blackness.

'Oh, no!'

Now he recalled what it was: a blind passage, called 'Turks' Alley', that ended in a tumbledown wall. The far side of the barrier was another quiet street, opening eventually into the centre of Camden Town, only a hundred metres from the Underground Station and a dozen bus-stops.

'Gotcher!' boomed a voice from behind him.

John spun on his heel, and saw that the dark mouth of the alley behind him was blocked by a bulky shape of menacing blackness.

A shape that began to advance slowly towards him, the stride slow and measured, confident that there was no escape.

John backed away, biting his lip. Now he was really in it. What his dad, his *real* father, called being at the end of the runway with no lift-off. His heel caught something and the boy stumbled. He peered down and saw a pile of abandoned blue plastic milk-crates jumbled at the bottom of the wall.

'Lift-off,' he whispered to himself.

It took him only a few seconds to pile the crates, one on top of another. He fumbled his way up them, feeling the rough stones on the crest of the wall.

'Hey! You better not try anything, son!' bellowed the voice.

The half-dozen spray-cans of coloured paint clattered together in John's rucksack as he swung himself up on top of the wall. A hand brushed at his ankle, then he was up and over, landing lightly on the far side. He jogged towards the centre and safety.

The policeman's head appeared over the wall, but the constable wasn't able to keep his balance and pull himself over it. He watched the tall black youth vanishing. At the turning, John paused and waved to the angry policeman. He didn't wave back.

'Cheeky young bleeder,' he muttered. 'I'll get you. One day. That's a promise.'

Kim Webber, formerly Greene, glanced at her wrist-watch. It was coming on towards ten o'clock, well over an hour past the time that John had been told to come home. Her husband, Mike, had gone round the corner to the pub, but he'd said he was going to be back before ten to watch the darts on the telly, and if John *still* wasn't home . . .

Kim was just thirty years old and she worked part-time as a secretary at the local junior school. Since the birth of little Norma-Jean four months ago, it had been harder to cope. A neighbour looked after the baby while Kim was at work, but that meant more housekeeping money dribbling away. She was seriously thinking about packing the job in next term, but she was worried about what Mike might say. Money had been tight in their cramped, two bedroomed flat at Beacon Hill, within stone-throwing distance of Holloway Prison. Mike had been made redundant only a couple of weeks after they were married and, despite all his efforts, had only just got work in the last month. He was a skilled plumber and he'd done courses at night school, but it had been the old story of racial prejudice when he went after work.

And that was something Kim knew plenty about.

Her own mother had come to England on a cold winter's day in 1955, off the boat from Trinidad, after a dreadful crossing with the long, sullen Atlantic rollers pitching and heaving. It had been snowing, something that John's Granny had never seen before. But it had still seemed like the promised land. A land that promised the chance of wealth and jobs after the poverty in the West Indies.

'Promised land,' said Kimberley to herself, tasting the sour words on her tongue. She hadn't seen much promise in her life.

She heard feet running up the quiet little street and she half-rose from her chair. The fish fingers already lay in the grill pan and the oven-ready chips were ready in the oven. If only John could get home before his . . . she hesitated . . . his stepfather.

But the feet ran on by.

Norma-Jean whimpered in her cot and Kim sighed. It was one of those dull evenings when she eased open the door at the back of her mind and peered in to question whether her second marriage was all she'd hoped. John's real father, Ben Greene, was a talented engineer, who'd also found the colour of his skin sometimes made work hard to come by. He was a decent man and now, looking back, Kim couldn't really remember why it was that they'd finally split up. He hadn't beaten her, hadn't been unfaithful, hadn't been a drinker. He'd worried a lot about money, but that was all right.

It was just that they'd somehow drifted apart. Ten

years of marriage ending not with a bang and not even with a whimper. Just drifting apart.

Kim had the radio on quietly, the last song before the news at ten: Elvis singing one of his best, 'You Were Always On My Mind.'

Kim sang along, the line about not holding you all the lonely times. Tears were very close.

There was the sound of feet coming round the side of the big old house, towards the back door of their flat. She hoped it was her son and not her husband. It meant a bit less trouble between them.

The door opened. 'Hi, Mum,' said John, wondering why his mother stood up and hugged him quite so hard.

By the time that Michael Webber came in from the pub, John was in his own room, supper finished, listening to the latest Run DMC album on his head-phones. The rucksack with the incriminating aerosol cans of spray paint was safely hidden under some sacks in the dusty old conservatory at the side of their flat.

'What time you get in, boy?'

John pretended he couldn't hear, looking up at the face framed in the doorway, miming deafness and shrugging his shoulders.

'Take them things off. I asked you what time you got in?'

'Didn't notice.' The music seeping from the ear-phones was crackling and tinny.

'Turn it off. Off, John!'

The boy could catch the scent of beer on his stepfather's breath. Michael Webber was a big man, seeming to fill the cramped room. He looked round as if he wanted somewhere to sit down, then decided that he'd do better to keep standing.

'What d'you want, Michael?' asked John, reaching across with his left hand to press the 'Stop' button on the music centre.

'I want . . . I wish you'd call me "Dad", and not Michael, son.'

'I'm not your son, and you aren't my father. I'm not goin' to pretend, *Mister* Webber.'

The man took a half-step forwards and John flinched, expecting a slap around the head. It wouldn't be the first time his stepfather had clipped him for being cheeky. But Mike Webber regained control and moved to the door. He paused and looked back over his shoulder at the sullen-faced teenager.

'You think bein' thirteen makes you king of the heap, John, but it don't. I know that you love Ben, and that's . . . But I'm married to your mum now and that makes me sort of father to you.'

John didn't answer until the door of his room had closed behind the burly figure. Then he whispered to himself: 'No, you aren't. Not now and not never.'

It was still humid, close to midnight.

The casement window was stiff as John tried to quietly ease it further open. He leant on the peeling cream paint, breathing deeply. He was only wearing pyjama bottoms but he was uncomfortably hot. There

13

wasn't a breath of wind all across North London. Somewhere towards Tufnell Park he could hear the distant rumble of angry thunder. The endless bass sound of the traffic on Camden Road and Hillmarton Road was a permanent counterpoint to John Greene's life, never stopping all through the night.

The boy hoped that it wasn't going to rain tomorrow. Now they were so close to the end of the summer term at his comprehensive school, they were playing lots of sport. Apart from his art, that was John's favourite subject.

On Sunday he'd be able to go and visit his father, who lived in a bed-sit out at Bounds Green, near the North Circular. They'd maybe go and watch a cricket match somewhere. John's dad had promised him that he'd try and get him into a team when he was fifteen.

He was already the youngest player in the school team; batting at number four and averaging over forty runs for the season. Some man had appeared a couple of times to ask if he was interested in playing for a North London representational team, but John wasn't that keen yet on moving away from his mates.

A natural left-hander, John had also been picking up some spectacular catches fielding at first slip. As he stared out into the warm, blank night, he smiled to himself as he remembered his best innings: coming in with two wickets down for only seven runs against some snobby Hampstead school, hitting eighty-five runs in less than an hour, including a steepling six, right into the pavilion.

The thunder was coming closer and he glimpsed

the torn silver lace of lightning, forking to earth. He recognized the agonized wailing of a fire-engine's siren, belting along towards Camden Town. That made him think of his narrow escape from the police, for what they called 'graffiti' or 'vandalism', but he and his friends called 'spray-can art'.

He signed his own wall-work with his tag, 'Inx'. A name that also appeared on his school work-folders.

There was a shout from one of the flats upstairs where a really weird couple of women lived. They were always having rows and breaking plates. Once a saucepan had come clean through their window and smashed in the garden, just missing the landlady's pet spaniel.

John looked down at his watch, angling its face to catch the orange glow of the street-lights. It was twenty past twelve. The air was stifling and he still didn't think he'd sleep. Maybe if he flicked around the dial of his radio there might be something to listen to.

There was a continental station that played old thirties' and forties' jazz records. John's other great musical love was that period, especially the songs of Billie Holiday. He left the window open and switched on the music centre, kneeling on the floor and keeping the volume very low. After everything else, it would be a perfect end to a perfect day if he woke up his mother and Michael.

There was a lot of static, crackling and hissing in his ears as he delicately turned the dial. A burst of

15

some language that sounded like two old men trying to be sick. Maybe it was Polish or Flemish.

Then there was a steady tone and a voice saying: 'Alpha Bravo Papa . . . Come in Alpha Bravo Papa.' It had to be a police wavelength.

A slow ballad, in what he recognized was French, followed. John kept moving the dial along.

'. . . the rookie's jammed the batter . . .'

A great surge of electronic garbage swamped the radio. 'What was that?' said the boy, trying to find the broadcast again. The voice had definitely been American.

The storm was sweeping nearer, bringing a breeze with it that tugged at the threadbare curtains of John's room. The radio reception was growing worse by the minute.

'Long ball down the power alley has . . .'

There it was again. John moved the thin green line backwards and forwards, a millimetre at a time, trying to stabilize the broadcast.

'Strawberry hits a low liner into deep centrefield and that's going to score Hernandez. McGee throws home to Pena and Tony gets the tag on Backman and looks for the double play at second. But Strawberry's gotten safely on the bag.'

There was a dazzling flash of lightning that seemed like it had exploded in the back garden. The air filled with the deafening crash of thunder, following right on top of the white light. John jumped, hand jerking the radio dial so that he lost the mysterious sports commentary. There was the pattering of heavy rain on the dusty flagstones and he hastily closed his window, noticing that the air seemed to smell funny and sharp, like the salt you could taste at the seaside.

He heard the thin, weak sound of his little baby sister, woken by the storm, crying in her cot in the other bedroom. John climbed into his own bed, wondering what that broadcast had been in the American voice.

'Baseball?' he wondered. Not that he knew anything about it. All he knew was that it was some soft kind of rounders.

Eventually the rhythm of the rain lulled him into sleep.

'Rounders! Oh, come on, sir, that's real evil. It's a girls' game, innit?'

But Mr Keaton, known as 'Buster', wasn't to be swayed. He was the head of boys' PE at the school. Indeed, he'd held that position for the last eighteen years, through rain and shine. His boast, often repeated, was that he'd 'seen the hard cases come and seen them go'. The day that using the slipper was banned was one of the saddest of Buster Keaton's career.

'I said we'd play rounders, and rounders is what we shall play. So, gentlemen, let us have no more of this palaver.'

'Can't we play cricket, sir?' begged John Greene, unhappily.

The teacher had a soft spot for the tall, well-built boy, admiring his natural talent for all games involving ball skills. With two more years to go, Mr Keaton had every hope that John would eventually captain the school cricket team and lead them to success. And there was also the lad's talent in other games; he was already playing for the school at basketball and volley-ball. Because of this he answered John far more gently than he might have done other boys.

'I'm afraid not, John. New policy from the Boss. Girls are playing cricket today.'

As he'd expected, this announcement brought an even louder chorus of moans from the group of third years.

'Girls!'

'That's a waste of time lettin' them play cricket, sir.'

'Bleedin' stupid,' muttered someone, but the teacher couldn't identify the voice.

'All right! That's enough!' A downcast silence surrounded him. 'I'm not saying what I think about this, but if our Headmaster says do it, then I do it. And if I do it, then so do you. Is that clear, all of you? Walters? Smallbrook? Right then, we play rounders.'

It took all of Buster's experience to control the boys for the afternoon. Fortunately, there was a school third year cricket match coming on Saturday and several of the lads were due to play. They were brought in line with threats of being dropped and the rest toed the mark under the lash of his tongue.

'You said something about this being for girls, Walters? How come you keep missing the ball if it's that easy?'

'Bat's too small.'

'You want a baseball bat, lad? Get on with it. Hand-eye co-ordination, just like cricket. Give it plenty of welly. Hit through the ball. Have another go at it.'

He was interrupted by John Greene, tugging at the sleeve of his maroon tracksuit.

'What?'

'Kid.'

'What?'

'Kid there, looks like he's wantin' to speak to you, sir.'

'Where? Oh, yes. Must be the American boy. He was due here this morning but I had a message. Something about . . . Never mind. Come here!'

The class all stopped, staring at the newcomer. He was a white boy, around the same height as John, five feet ten, broad-shouldered, with an easy, athletic walk. Just over ten and a half stone. He had a shock of blond hair that looked like it got expensively cut at least once a fortnight. He was wearing brown leather brogues and turned up black 501 jeans. They could see a plain white T-shirt partly covered with a dark blue satin jacket with lettering on it. There was a gust of wind, blowing a cloud of dust across the sports field. The boy half-turned away and John read 'New York Yankees' across the back of the jacket. He knew that they were a famous baseball team and it crossed his mind how odd it was that suddenly he seemed to see and hear about baseball at every turn.

'You are Richard Okie,' said Mr Keaton, beckoning the boy to join them.

'Affirmative, sir.'

The reply brought a burst of laughter from the listening English boys. The teacher turned slowly to rake them with a chilling glance. 'Forgive them, Okie. They are laughing with glee at the prospect of each doing four laps of the field, culminating in fifty push-ups. Off you go, lads.'

As he jogged along, John kept glancing at the American boy. His form teacher, Miss Levine, had mentioned that the kid was going to join them. His father was some sort of big wheel in the American Air Force, stationed out in Suffolk, who was working with a local engineering factory for a month and had brought his son to experience English education.

John was looking forward to talking to the Yank kid. His dad had worked for a few months in the States and had told John tales of it being a great country for opportunities, where, most places, people only worried about how good you were at your job and didn't blank you out because they thought your skin happened to be the wrong colour.

John had also become interested in the game of American Football, watching it on Channel Four on Sundays and Tuesdays during the winter. He supported the New York Giants and wanted to ask Richard Okie if he'd ever seen them play.

Once the four laps were over and the press-ups completed, Mr Keaton got them organized to play rounders.

In a peculiar way, the presence of the stranger made all the English boys want to try harder to do well, and the game went on with a surprising intensity. John was named captain of one team, and a tall skinhead boy, Kenny Ravven, picked the other. Kenny was in John's class and was excellent at games, but he was

21

also a born stirrer of trouble. His nickname at the school was 'Ravin' Ravven'.

Richard Okie was left over at the end of the selection and Buster Keaton called John over. 'Take Richard in your team and explain the rules to him, will you?'

'Yes, sir. Come on.'

The American boy stopped him, offering him his hand. 'Pleased to meet you. I'm Richard William Okie Junior. I like to be called Rick.'

'Hello, Rick. Welcome to school. I'm John Elijah Greene and I'm called John.'

Rick gave him a broad grin, shaking hands firmly. 'Good to meet you, John. Let's go play ball.'

Rounders wasn't one of John's favourite games. He'd played it at Junior School, but he found it a bit boring, and the bat was far too small. But he became involved in that afternoon's match, cheering his team on at the bat, and encouraging them in the field. Ravven's side batted first and Rick Okie distinguished himself with a good diving catch and a couple of smart pieces of run-saving.

'What number do you want to bat, Rick?'

'Back home at baseball I normally go in three. But you're the skipper, John. Put me where you like, and I'll go for the big hit into the bleachers.'

'What?'

The boy grinned again. 'Good old Yankee saying, John. Don't let it worry you.'

During the opening part of the game the cloudless

sky had become smeared with dark grey, swooping in from the west on a rising wind. From the look of it, they were about to get rained on. John hoped that he'd have at least one chance of batting before the storm broke.

He'd decided to go in first, wanting to hit a rounder and reduce the deficit on Ravven's team.

After becoming so used to a cricket bat, the rounders bat felt ridiculously short and light in his left hand.

'Go, John!' yelled someone.

The ball was tossed in at him and he swung, catching it near the end of the bat, feeling the sweet contact. The ball went soaring away, far over the heads of the fielders, bouncing into a patch of thistles near the overgrown long-jump pit.

'Well played,' said Buster Keaton as the boy ran past him to score an easy rounder.

The next boy failed to connect and the American came up third. John had briefed him on the rules, which, Rick commented, were a lot like baseball.

'Show us how it's done, Flash,' yelled Kenny Ravven. 'Maybe you can play for the right team next, 'stead of that lot!'

'I'll look forward to seeing you in my room at five minutes to nine tomorrow, Ravven,' said Mr Keaton, his thin lips showing his anger.

Rick turned to John, the rounders bat dangling from his hand. 'I don't get it. What's that about? Why his team?'

'Ain't you noticed, mate?' said Joe Taylor, a short, stocky friend of John.

The American boy looked puzzled. 'No. I don't get it.' He hesitated. 'Unless he means that nearly all his team . . .'

'Are white kids,' finished Joe. 'Right. Most of this team aren't. Geddit?'

Rick nodded slowly. 'Sure. Sure, I get it fine.'

He stepped up to take strike, holding the bat loosely in both hands. 'Could do with a mite longer handle,' he said.

'You only use one hand, you stupid . . .' began Kenny, who was ready to bowl the ball. Checking himself when he caught Buster Keaton's eye on him.

'Guess I'll use two hands. If'n it's not 'gainst any rules.'

'I think you could possibly find it easier to only use one hand, Richard,' suggested the games master.

'I'll give it a go like this, if I may, sir?'

'Go on, then,' said Mr Keaton, waving his hand for Kenny to pitch.

John studied the American boy's stance, seeing how he stood side-on, looking awkward and bunched-up with both hands gripping the short handle. The tip of the bat swung right back until it almost touched the blond curls.

'Ready, Goldilocks?' sneered Kenny Ravven, getting a toadying snigger from his mates.

Rick didn't answer him, waiting patiently for the ball.

The first heavy drops of rain were beginning to fall,

plopping noisily on the dusty leaves of the plane trees along the edge of the field.

Kenny threw and Rick Okie swung. It was a strange, punching sort of shot, not like any rounders hit that any of them had ever seen. There was a lot of hip and shoulder in the blow, as well as enormous power from the wrists. The crack of bat striking ball was loud and clean.

'Lift-off,' whispered John Greene. His eye just able to follow the blur of the rounders ball as it flew up and away.

And up and away and away, vanishing over the privet hedge that guarded the right side of the school playing-field.

'Lucky fluke,' said Kenny, convincing nobody, not even himself.

'Good shot, son,' said Mr Keaton appreciatively. 'If you can hit a cricket ball that well, then we might find a place for you in the school team. Don't you think so, John?'

He nodded, grinning widely at the amazing hit, and the expression of shock on Kenny Ravven's face. 'Yes, sir,' he replied.

Playing rounders instead of cricket hadn't turned out so bad, after all.

4 Miss Levine called John out next morning, at register. 'I hear from Mr Keaton that you and our American friend there succeeded in hitting it off rather well at games yesterday?'

'Yes, miss.'

She had a small, neat, round face, with pale blue eyes almost hidden behind thick-lensed spectacles.

'You can smile if I make a joke about "hitting", John, if you wish.'

'Yes, Miss Levine,' he smiled.

'Richard is with us until the end of this term, which is blissfully close. He will sit in on all our lessons, though he will obviously have been doing work of quite different kinds and standards. For a couple of weeks this won't much matter.'

'No, miss.'

'Since you share an interest in foolish, time-wasting activities like games, I can think of nobody better to look after Richard. If you don't mind, John?'

He bit his lip. If he was going to have to nursemaid the Yank kid around, it was going to slow down his own social life. Then the image of that marvellous, bizarre rounders hit came to him, overlaid with the shocked expression on Kenny Ravven's face.

'No, miss. Don't mind.'

She nodded, looking pleased. 'Thank you, John. Mr Saunders asked me if I knew someone I could trust and I thought of you.'

Mr Saunders, known as 'Goofy', was the new head of the comprehensive, who'd only come to the school at the beginning of the summer term and was already showing himself to be a lot more strict than his predecessor.

Miss Levine curled her finger, beckoning Rick Okie to join John at her desk. 'You two have already met.'

'Yes, ma'am.'

'I think "miss" sounds better here than "ma'am", Richard.'

'Sorry, ma'am. I mean, sorry, miss.'

'Go and sit next to John. And follow him, within reasonable bounds, everywhere he goes.'

'What if I want to go to the . . . ?' began John, nudging the American boy.

'I said "within reasonable bounds", John Greene. And we both know what we mean. Go and sit down.'

As they went to the desk at the back of the room, they passed Kenny Ravven, who muttered something to Rick Okie. The boy checked his stride, then carried on and sat down by John.

'What'd that nutter say to you, Rick?'

'He . . . nothing really.'

'Yeah,' said John, knowing what 'nothing' meant.

The day slipped by without any noteworthy incidents. Rick was amazed at the state of the school's buildings, with chipped woodwork and peeling paint, and the lack of textbooks for all the pupils also puzzled him.

'How come your parents don't buy 'em for you, John?' he asked.

'First off, they're not supposed to and second off, they couldn't afford them anyway.'

Judy Harvey, a tall girl with braided, beaded hair, overheard the conversation. 'You got some nasty shocks comin', Goldilocks, haven't you?'

'Guess so,' he replied. 'I surely guess so.'

At lunch-time, all third years were supposed to stay on the school's premises and either have the official dinner or bring a packed meal. John, like most of his friends, didn't do either, having convinced his mother that they were allowed to go to the chippy, a quarter of a mile away. Rick hadn't brought any food or money, so John offered him half his fish and chips.

'Hey, this is real good, John. I've been over here in England with Dad a coupla months and this is the first time I've eaten real English fish and french fries. I mean chips. They're real good.'

They sat down and ate them, washed down with a can of Coke, near a fountain at the edge of the shopping precinct, keeping a careful eye open for any patrolling teachers. While they ate, they talked a little about themselves.

Rick asked John why he didn't go home for lunch.

'Too far. This isn't the nearest place to where I live. That's by Holloway nick.'

'What's a nick?'

'Federal penitentiary. Prison. I had . . . kind of a bit of trouble at my old school, that was nearer. So I came here half-way through my first year.'

'First year? You're thirteen, like me. So back home you'd be in the Seventh Grade at Junior High School. Like I am back in Utica.'

'Where's that?'

'New York State.'

'Near the Statue of Liberty and the Empire State? You watch the Giants play gridiron?'

The boy laughed, showing the most amazingly perfect set of gleaming white teeth that John Greene had ever seen. 'Hey, my man! Utica's around two hundred miles away from the Big Apple. That's New York City. But I've seen all the tourist stuff. And an uncle's got a season ticket for the Giants.'

'You seen Lawrence Taylor play?'

'I've seen LT knock guys half-way out of the stadium. He's the best.'

The talk shifted briefly to cricket. Rick Okie was fascinated that games went on for five days. 'And then a lotta times they just end in a draw? Is that right?'

John nodded. 'Yeah. But there's a lot of real skill in the game.'

'My uncle says that a drawn game is as exciting as kissing your own sister.'

Both boys laughed at the image.

'You're a batter? You don't pitch? Or do you call them a thrower?'

'Bowler,' corrected John. 'No, I bat. And I'm not bad at fieldin' either.'

'I saw that when we played that softball. You ought to try out for baseball, John. My father runs the team on the Air Force base. I could borrow some gear, bring it in the last week. Would the guys like to give it a go?'

'I would. Probably most of 'em would. Buster's the man to ask.'

'That Mr Keaton? Buster, like the old movie comic? Like it. I'll ask him.'

John crumpled up the paper and threw it neatly into the nearest waste-basket. The two boys began the walk back to the school.

'Your mum over here as well?'

'In England? No. She's back in Encino.'

'Where's that?'

'California. North part of LA. You know?'

John stopped. 'I know Los Angeles. But I thought you said you lived in New York State.'

'That's me and my father. My parents separated 'bout four years ago. I live six months with each of them. Right now it's Dad's turn.'

'Is that all right?'

'I'm sorry? How d'you mean, John?'

'Well, my mum and dad split up, and she's married again. But I don't . . . we don't . . . I don't get on with him.'

'I've got friends with that problem. Whose fault is it, John?'

'His,' he replied instantly, without even thinking about it. In fact, it was a question that he'd *never* really thought much about. 'Well, it's me as well, I suppose. But, we just don't get on at all. I want to live with me dad, but he's not got room for me. Not yet, anyway.'

There was an unusually relaxed atmosphere at the school with the holidays beckoning from just around the corner. Homework had almost disappeared and even the toughest teachers eased up. John found that he was enjoying the company of the straw-haired American boy, though he had to endure some teasing from several of his friends.

Before the last double lesson, which was English, Joe Taylor sidled up to John. 'Goin' t'do a piece tonight, Inx?'

'Can't. Mum and him are goin' out to his sister's. Gotta watch the baby.'

'Tomorrow?'

'Sure.'

'What 'bout Goldilocks?'

Rick shook his head. 'I'm not sure I like that name.'

'What you goin' t'do 'bout it?'

The two boys faced up to each other. John pushed his way between them. 'Come on, Joe, lay off him. He's all right.' Turning to the American. 'And you gotta take it easy. Don't let 'em get to you. Specially Ravin' Ravven and his skinhead mates.'

'Yeah,' said Rick. 'Guess you're right, John. Sorry, Joe.' He offered his hand to shake. Looking a little surprised, the stocky black teenager shook it.

'All right, Rick. Tomorrow then, Inx?'

'Sure.'

As he sat down, Rick looked at John. 'What's with the name "Inx"? Huh? And going to do a piece. What's that mean?'

'It's my tag.'

'Like on your folder there?'

'Right. You must've seen all the spray-can art on the underground trains in New York. That's the kind of stuff we do. We call it doing a piece. Like a piece of street art.'

'Hey, that's right. I tell you, John, if you meet my father you better not mention doing all that graffiti stuff. Not unless you want to see a human head explode in front of you.'

'Bit against it, is he?'

'Like Nero was against Christians! My old man's a few paces further right than Ronald Reagan. That means waaaaaaay out in right field. Vandals should be jailed! That's what he figures.'

'It's not vandalism; it's a beautiful crime. That's what I read somewhere. We only do it on empty, wrecked buildings. Can't make 'em look worse.'

'What'd your father think 'bout it?'

John sniffed. 'My real dad'd probably think it was all right. My stepfather and your old man sound like they'd get on well.'

The conversation was cut off by the inevitably late arrival of their teacher.

Piggy Blunt was one of those men who look thirty going on sixty and are incapable of ever getting anywhere on time. Mr Blunt's progress through the corridors of the comprehensive was always marked by

32

a trail of fallen papers and dropped books. He peered at the world over smeared half-moon glasses and never seemed to lose a puckered, disapproving kind of frown.

'Sit down shut up don't shuffle open your books at page forty-nine begin reading at the barge she sat in stop giggling.'

The lesson, carrying them through the mid-part of Antony and Cleopatra, seemed to last for ever.

But the bell finally released them into the late afternoon sunshine.

'Fancy a Coke, John?'

'Got to get home. Told you, I've got to baby-sit for Norma-Jean.'

'That your sister's name?' The two boys were surrounded by hundreds of children, surging away down the wide main drive of the comprehensive.

'Yes. Why? Somethin' wrong with it?'

'Course not. It was Marilyn Monroe's real name. Bet you didn't know that.'

John shrugged his shoulders, stepping to one side and narrowly avoiding being mown down by a pair of first year girls on BMX bikes.

'Course I did. My . . . my stepfather's a sort of Marilyn freak. Got dozens of books and vids of her films and posters and . . . and everything. That's why he had her christened that name.'

They reached the main road and both hesitated. Rick looked at his watch, a flashy red, white and blue Swatch. 'It's not four yet. Dad's got this apartment only a coupla blocks from here. When you got to be home?'

'Not until six. But I've got to get some shopping on the way.'

John didn't need a lot of persuading.

At the corner they saw Kenny Ravven, but when he spotted them walking towards him he looked the other way and crossed over the road.

'Typical that,' said John. 'Get him with his mates and he reckons he's really Jack-the-lad. On his own he's nothin'.'

'Who's this Jack person?'

'Means a dude who fancies himself. My grandfather used to say it.'

Rick nodded his understanding. 'John? Were your parents born in England?'

'Course. Why?'

'Grandparents?'

'Two were and two weren't. Two were already here and two came over from the West Indies. Why d'you ask?'

'Just that we're kind of similar, you and me. My mother's parent's were both born in the States, in wind-washed Wisconsin. But my dad's parents came from Czechoslovakia. Real name was Okovitz. See what I mean about being the same?'

The building was part of an undistinguished North London terrace in yellowish-grey bricks, the window frames rotting, split into several separate flats. Rick pulled out a key and led the way up to the second floor. The front door was newly-painted and rein-forced. A neat white card in a thin brass frame read: 'Master-Sergeant Richard W. Okie Snr. Ring and Wait.'

There was a double-lock on the door. John noticed that one of the keys carried a dark blue plastic tag with the initials 'USAAF' on it.

'Hey, it's really . . . What a great place, Rick. Dead cool. Does this belong to your father?'

Rick peeled off the New York Yankees jacket and dropped it on the sofa. 'Course not. It's an Air Force apartment. Dad's using it while he's working on this radar guidance gizmo with one of your local firms. Kind of neat though, isn't it?'

John knew that 'neat' meant really nice. But he also thought he'd never seen such a neat and immaculate place. It looked like the sun had to wipe its feet before it came through a window and any dust had to report for rapid departure every hour on the hour. Nothing was out of place or out of line.

The furniture almost squeaked with newness and everything glittered with polish. A huge colour photo of a massive American bomber dominated one wall. Beneath it was a sideboard with several smaller photos in ordered ranks. A brand-new colour telly and two videos loomed out of a corner near a well-stocked bar. A glass bowl of popcorn was perfectly positioned in the middle of a round table by a door that led through to a corridor beyond.

'I'll go get us a couple of Cokes from the kitchen, John.'

'Thanks. But I gotta go soon, Rick. Don't want any more hassle from Mum and her . . . and him.'

'Sure thing. You got it, John. I have to take a leak first. Didn't fancy using the rest-rooms at the school.'

'Don't blame you. Don't call 'em bogs for nothing, do they.'

Rick stuck his head back through the door. 'Oh. You aren't CND are you?'

'Well, not officially joined up, but I think they've got the right . . .'

'No! For both our sakes, don't say that. Please, John! Dad's real touchy over that. Anyway, I'll get the drinks.'

He vanished and John wandered over and picked up one of the pictures on the sideboard. It was a photo of Rick holding a fishing-rod.

He didn't hear the front door open. First warning that he wasn't alone came when a hand the size of a side of beef lifted him clear off the floor and a voice shouted in his ear: 'Gotcha! Who the heck are you and what the heck are you doing here? You got two seconds 'fore I ring your neck like a Thanksgiving turkey!!'

5 'I'm real sorry, John. Real sorry. Here, let me go get you another can of Coke?'

'Thanks, Mr Okie, but I really ought to be gettin' home. Got to do some shopping for my mother on the way. Thanks, though.'

He stood up, wiping his hands nervously down the sides of his trousers. Master-Sergeant Richard William Okie Senior also stood up, his immense size hanging over the boy like the face of a cliff. John guessed that Rick's father had to be around six feet tall, weighing in over the sixteen stone mark. His Air Force uniform was immaculately pressed, the row of medal ribbons splashed across the left side of his chest.

He'd apologized endlessly after Rick had come in from the kitchen and found his new friend dangling inches off the floor in his father's grip.

'Lotta walk-in robberies round here, John. Daytime too. Saw you and thought . . . Gee, but I'm so sorry and . . . Richard Junior just starting school. I didn't really think you . . .'

Rick mentioned to his father that John could be good at baseball and the big man's bright blue eyes lit up.

37

'Then he just gotta come out t'the base and play some ball.'

'That's why it's called baseball, Mr Okie? Because it's played on Air Force bases?'

The room trembled at the rumbling bellow of laughter from the American. 'That *is* a good one, John. That honest and truly is. But I mean it. Soon as semester's done you can come up with Richard Junior.'

'They call them terms, not semesters over here, Dad. I'm going to ask the games teacher about bringing in some equipment in the last few days and showing the guys a little about baseball. Is that all right with you?'

'Why, for sure, son. For sure.'

John edged cautiously towards the door, noticing that he'd been sitting on a small check scatter cushion and it was all crumpled. He felt sure that the moment he was gone the Master Sergeant would leap upon it and wrestle it back into impeccable neatness.

'Got to go. Thanks for the Coke. Nice to meet you, Mr Okie. See you at school tomorrow, Rick. Bye.'

Only when he was back out in the street did he remember that Rick had asked him not to call him 'Rick' in front of his father, who insisted on Richard Junior for him.

Baby-sitting was boring.

All he had to do was put a sticky mess in one end of his little sister, and then clean up when it came out the other end.

He spent some of the time planning his next piece. It was going to mean laying out for a couple of fresh cans of spray-paint, so the five pounds for tonight's sitting would come in useful. There was a derelict row of shops only a quarter mile from Finsbury Park tube station, and they'd agreed to give it something special.

One of his mates had got hold of all four of the *Jaws* films on video and they'd watched them all through, one after another. It had given John the idea for his main piece. Using a soft pencil he sketched it out, listening for any whimpering from Norma-Jean which might mean one end or the other needed servicing. But she was sleeping contentedly in his mother's room. He took a chance and put on one of his favourite Billie Holiday albums, electing the track from the very end of her tragic career. When her voice was shot and her timing unsteady, but she got by on soul.

'For all we know, we may never meet again,' came easing out, the volume set way down low.

The shape of the great white shark began to appear on the paper, jaws gaping, rows of teeth sharply serrated, darkly tipped. John used all his skill as an artist to make the predator look as if it was bursting off the page, emerging from the sea, waves boiling whitely about it. Wall-art needed exotic, swirling lettering and he carefully pencilled in the word: 'JAWZ' to the side of the shark. He thought it was a bit corny, but it should work on the wall when the spray-can team started on it tomorrow. Tongue licking the corner of his lips, the boy added his tag, 'Inx', at the bottom left of the sketch for the piece.

The ringing of the phone made him jump and he darted to answer it, before it woke his baby sister. He gave the number and listened.

'That you, John?'

'Yeah. Hi, Dad.'

'Wish you'd call me "Ben" rather than "Dad", John. You know how it upsets Mike and your mother.'

'Mr Webber and Mum're out tonight, Dad. I'm sitting for Norma-Jean.'

'And don't call Mike . . . Oh, forget it, son. Listen, I really rang to talk to you. Find out if I'm goin' to see you during the hols?'

'Yeah.' Too eager he thought, trying to sound more cool. 'Yeah, Dad, that'd be good. I don't have any other plans.'

'Kim said . . . Your mother said she was going with Mike and their baby to a rented caravan at Clacton for a fortnight. But she thought you wouldn't sort of want to go with 'em.'

'No. No, I don't.'

His father sounded a bit odd. A bit strained, John thought.

'Well . . . looks like somethin' might be comin' up. *Might* be.'

'Holiday?'

'Sort of. Well, no, not exactly. Oh, blast it and . . .' The pips drowned out the next few words and John heard the chinking sound of another coin rattling into the box. 'Just made it. Look. Can't talk long. There's a crowd waitin' to use the phone. But I'll tell you in a couple of days when I got more news. More definite sort of news.'

'But where's the holiday goin' t'be, Dad?'

There was a terrible crackling and hissing on the line and John could barely hear what his father was saying. 'Not . . . Southern . . . good job and they reckon I could easily . . . with me if you . . . It'd be a big break though.'

'What? What'd be a big break, Dad? I didn't hear what you said. Oh, no. Norma-Jean's woken up and started bawling. Dad! Tell me again . . .'

'Must go, John, my boy. But the weather is . . . Angeles . . . your mother. Lots of love, son. See you very soon.'

The pips cut off any further talk and John slowly replaced the receiver on its rest. He picked up his baby sister and walked her round the small flat to try and calm her crying. He puzzled over the mysterious call. Had his father said 'angels'? Or had he said 'Angeles'?

As in, Los Angeles.

When John's mother and stepfather came home, just before midnight, they seemed much happier than he'd seen them for a long time. Mum was smiling and telling him about the family and how she'd enjoyed the break and the chance to get out of the flat for a bit. Mike gave him a fiver and Mum took a New York Seltzer – his favourite black cherry flavour – out of

41

her bag. She kissed him and thanked him for looking after Norma-Jean.

They didn't ask whether there'd been any phone calls, and he decided not to tell them about the odd, garbled message from his father.

Rick Okie asked Mr Keaton whether he could bring in some of the equipment for baseball before the end of term. The games teacher was keen on the idea and it was agreed that they'd do it on the last Wednesday of the final week. Rick's father said he'd bring along the gear, and even offered to stay and help out, but Rick put him off, saying he'd rather do it on his own.

The days flew by and it seemed as though the sun shone all the time. John found that he was getting on a bit better with his mother's husband, which made the atmosphere in the Beacon Hill flat a whole lot happier.

It was odd, but it had been the American boy's question that had triggered the change in John's thinking about the relationship. Until then he'd never honestly given it much thought. The split between his parents had been desperately hurtful and he'd believed for some time that it had all been his fault. Then he'd come to see that this wasn't true. But he had to blame someone for the break-up of the family unit, and who better than the cuckoo in their nest? The new 'father' who'd come and won his mother's affection? And if he and Mike didn't get on, then it certainly wasn't John's fault. It was nothing to do with him.

★

John found himself becoming good friends with Rick Okie. They went around a lot together at school, despite the sneering of Ravven and his toady friends. Several evenings, John joined Rick at the flat, watching videos or playing music. Rick's love was country-rock and his father had an amazing collection of early rock and roll albums. There was also a rack of videos of American Football games with titles like 'Great Quarterbacks' and 'Crunch Course'.

Master-Sergeant Okie was often busy at the factory, or commuting back to the Suffolk air-base. Twice, John, with his mother's permission, stayed overnight at the flat.

Rick came along on one of their spray-paint expeditions, even though he had absolutely no skill at all with the aerosols. But he was great at keeping watch for the local police patrols.

'JAWZ' worked out well and was greatly admired by everyone in the gang. It even got photographed in the local paper, along with the signature 'Inx' that was John Greene's own. It provoked letters in the local paper about whether it was vandalism or art, a subject that Miss Levine picked for a debate on the last Monday of term. She tried to get everyone involved in the discussion but John, suspecting some devious kind of teachers' trick, kept quiet.

One evening, John came home and found that his father was visiting, sitting in his old arm-chair, drinking coffee from the mug that John had bought him as a present from a junior school trip to Windsor Castle,

43

years ago. It had 'World's Best Dad' printed on the side in maroon lettering. John hadn't seen the mug for years and had thought it must have got lost when they moved. He was surprised at the jerk of pain he felt seeing Dad sitting there, Mum the other side of the room, the two of them laughing together. The baby was lying on her back on a white rug spread on the floor.

'Hello, Johnny,' said his father.

'You haven't called me that for ages.'

'No. Just felt like it. Being here with Kim and feeling cosy and like a family.'

'Ben,' said Mum, warningly. 'That's enough. Mike'll be back in a minute.'

'We're not doin' nothing wrong, Kim. Mike knows I'm here and he knows why. He was better pleased than anyone about John here and . . .'

'No,' snapped Mum. 'Not now, Ben. I mean it. There'll be big trouble 'tween you an' me. Wait till it's fixed for sure and definite. Then we'll tell John. That's what we all agreed. Then and not a moment before. You promised, Ben.'

John realized that his mother was trembling on the brink of tears. And he didn't know why.

What was it they were going to tell him when it was all fixed? His father had something tucked away that could be something good. There was a tone in his voice that almost reminded John of Christmas. An old Christmas, when everything was fine in the family, and his father had got a special secret present for one of them that he was dead pleased about.

But what was it now? What on earth was the special secret present?

Norma-Jean suddenly started to cry, sensing the tension in the room, and the moment passed.

At last it was the final week of term. The next day was the Wednesday, when Rick was going to show them all about the great game of baseball.

6

'Sorry I'm late, guys. Got snagged round Camden Town and then tried to hang a left into one of your one-way streets and then a patrolman came along and . . . well, I guess one damned thing just led to another.'

Sweat was running from the broad, tanned forehead of Master-Sergeant Richard William Okie Senior, of the United States of America Air Force, soaking into the uniform shirt, which already looked at least two sizes too small.

'Least he hasn't got his helmet and M16 carbine,' whispered Rick, fighting to hide his embarrassment.

Mr Keaton had watched the arrival of the glittering, vermilion Chevrolet pick-up truck with some amazement. He went over to shake the hand of the American, welcoming him to the school.

'Good of you to come, Sergeant Okie. Can the boys give you a hand with anything?'

'Good to meet you. Richard Junior's told me a lot about you, Buster.'

'Oh, no . . .' muttered Rick, trying to shrink himself to a centimetre high so he could hide behind a convenient blade of grass.

But the teacher didn't turn a hair at being addressed by his nickname. He merely called out for half a dozen

46

lads to help heave the three large hampers from the back of the truck.

'Sure you don't want me to stick around and lend a hand, Richard Junior?' bellowed Sergeant Okie. 'Be happy to oblige.'

'Thanks, Dad. It'll be fine. Can you come back around four?'

'Sixteen hundred hours ETA it is, son. Just so long as I can find my way round the highways here. It's like trying to motor around a rabbit warren. Don't you find that, Buster?'

'Can't say I do . . . Err, Richard. Can't say I do. Then again, I was born only a half mile down the road there, so I suppose I've absorbed my way around, so to speak.'

The Chevrolet roared off, spinning wheels and leaving a streak of scorched rubber along the school's main drive.

'Right, Rick,' said the teacher. 'Now, over to you. And, I think we'll go back to calling me *Mr* Keaton again, if you don't mind.'

'Sorry, sir.'

'Get on with it.'

John was impressed at the cool self-possession that the American boy showed, laying out the bases in a diamond shape, explaining all the time what he was doing, emptying the baskets of a jumble of bats and gloves and baseballs.

'Perhaps if you just give us a brief outline of the way the game is played, and then show us how all this

47

stuff is used afterwards?' suggested Mr Keaton to Rick.

'Then we can laugh at the bleedin' Yank cissy stuff,' sniggered Ravven.

'Think it's easy?' asked Rick, a bright spot of colour suddenly flaring on each cheek-bone.

'Course. Soppy great ball and big bat. Hit that clean over the rotten school, couldn't I?'

'Could you? Perhaps Kenneth could have first go, sir?'

'Perhaps,' smiled the games teacher. 'But first, a little about how the game works.'

'Baseball. A lightning description. All right, now listen good. It's a lot like your rounders . . . in some ways. The bases are like your posts, but they're a lot further apart.'

'How far?' asked John.

'Ninety feet. That's half as long again as a cricket pitch.'

'How big are the bats?' asked Mr Keaton.

'I got a picture of one of the all-time greats. Reggie Jackson, from the Oakland Athletics.' He handed it to John to pass around.

'That doesn't look like a bat,' laughed Joe Taylor, taking it next. 'Looks like somethin' he just uprooted out of a forest.'

'It is kind of big. Most bats weigh in around thirty-four ounces. Nearly two pounds.'

'How do you score?' asked one of Kenny Ravven's

48

gang, earning a dirty look from his leader for having the nerve to show any interest.

'Hey, in your rounders you only get a run if you hit the ball and run around *all* the bases without stopping. That right?'

'Yeah,' agreed Joe Taylor.

'In baseball you hit and run as far as you can. You can just go to first base and stop there. Then, when the next guy comes up to bat and hits it, you can run on further.'

Mr Keaton nodded. 'I see. So you can take as long as you like to get around. And I suppose you mustn't have two people on the same post. I mean, base? And when you get to fourth then you count a run?'

'Sure,' said Rick. 'We call it home plate, but that's the idea. Any questions, so far?'

'What's a homer?' asked Shane Harvey, Judy's twin brother.

'A what?' said Kenny Ravven in a squeaky, high voice. Trying for a cheap laugh and not getting it.

'I'll come to that in a moment,' replied Rick, ignoring the skinhead.

'What about the bowler?' asked Mr Keaton.

'The pitcher, sir. He throws the ball to the hitter. That white area I've marked off there is called home plate. Guy with the bat stands there, either this side or the other, depending on whether he's left or right-handed. Pitcher throws the ball over the home plate at a height between the batter's knees and his armpits. He does that without it being hit then that's called a strike.'

'Please don't try again with one of your so-called jokes about going on strike, Ravven,' said Mr Keaton, coldly.

'How many goes does he have?' asked John. He'd been looking through some of the pictures that Rick had brought along and found a great photo of a hitter called Dan Mattingly, wearing the New York Yankees' uniform and the number Twenty-Three. John was specially interested to see the man was batting left-handed. Suddenly, he felt he'd really like to have a go with one of the bats himself.

'Well, if he doesn't get the pitch over the plate then it's called a ball. Three strikes without a hit and the batter's out. If he gets four balls wide of the plate then he gets a free walk to the first base. Three batters out and the innings is closed. Most games run for seven innings each team. Oh, and if the hitter strikes the baseball behind him that's called foul and it doesn't count.'

'I think I understand that,' said Mr Keaton. 'I'm sure it'll all be clear once we start to play it. Certainly sounds quite like rounders in its basic approach.'

'It is,' replied Rick.

'What about hitting a homer?' asked Shane Harvey.

'Oh, for sure. If the hitter strikes the ball out over the wall around the park then it's called a home run and he gets to trot all the way round the bases to score a run, and bring in any of the other players from his team who were already on any of the bases. Get it?'

There was a general nodding of heads. Kenny Ravven went and picked up one of the bats, swinging it clumsily round his head. 'Yeah, like it. Could do some real damage in a row with this.'

'That's typical of you, Kenny,' said John, angrily. 'That's all that creeps like you think about. How you can do somethin' nasty to hurt someone.'

'Yeah? What you goin' . . . ?'

'Shut up, both of you,' said Keaton. 'Ravven, you should try engaging your brain before opening your mouth. Greene, I'm not disputing the rightness of your views, but this is not the time nor the place nor the way to express them. Any more and there'll be a couple of detentions. And I *do* know it's nearly the end of term. Let's get on with it, Rick.'

Apart from the bats, mostly junior size, and baseballs, Master-Sergeant Okie had sent them enough gear to fit out a regiment of players. Gloves of all kinds, for fielders and for the pitcher and catcher, who was like a wicket-keeper. The catcher also had a big padded chest-protector and face-mask.

'Is all this protection necessary?' asked Mr Keaton, trying on the mask.

'Good pitcher'll let her go around a hundred miles an hour. And if the ball just tips the bat and comes off at an angle, the catcher could get seriously hurt. That's why he has such a big glove as well.'

John was itching to get a go with the bat, but he didn't want to push forward and try and impose on his friendship with the American boy. So he deliberately waited at the back of the crowd.

After they'd all tried on the equipment, Buster

Keaton clapped his hands for quiet. 'All right, we haven't got as much time left as I'd like. Rick? What's the best way of doing this so that at least everyone gets a go with the bat?'

'Sure, Coach. I mean, sir. I hadn't realized time had gone so fast. Best might be if I do all the pitching and everyone gets at least one go at bat. Rest can field. I'll tell people where to go.'

It only took a couple of minutes for Rick to place boys in the correct fielding positions, explaining briefly what each of them had to do. He picked out John last of all.

'Seen you catch and throw. You play short-stop. It's normally the best and fastest fielder on the team. You gotta watch which base guys are running to. So's you can throw and get 'em out. And if the ball goes deep, then you have to act as relay to pass it on to the infielders.'

'I got it,' said John, feeling a surge of excitement, like he did whenever he was playing a game of any kind. It was almost as big a buzz as running from the law when you got caught doing a piece on some old building.

What amazed all the English boys was how hard it was to hit the baseball. After trying out the different sizes of bat, most people opted for the smaller, junior versions. Rick Okie was deliberately trying to pitch at them without putting any spin or dip on the ball, and everyone had half a dozen goes. But only one or two managed to make a hard, sweet contact.

Buster Keaton himself tried out with the bat, swinging so hard his sunglasses fell off the end of his nose.

'Goodness! It's jolly difficult, isn't it, Rick? I thought it would be a lot easier.'

'One of the finest hitters ever . . . guy called Ted Williams, played mainly for the Red Sox, said that striking the baseball with the bat was the single most skilled thing in any sport.'

'I think that could be an exaggeration,' said Mr Keaton, wiping a trickle of sweat from his gleaming forehead.

'Well, you gotta remember that the guys playing in the Leagues back home are the very best. They get paid good money to be the best. But even the top hitters rarely average more than three hits out of ten. That shows you how difficult it is. Suppose Jack Nicklaus only managed to hit the golf ball one time in three? See what I mean?'

The teacher nodded slowly. 'Yes. I suppose so. Must say I'd never thought about it. Now I've tried it myself I realize there's a very high degree of skill in it.'

'My go,' said John.

'No, it's my go,' interrupted Kenny Ravven, pushing forwards.

'John Greene's go,' said Rick quietly.

'Oh, yeah. You'd bleedin' say that, wouldn't you? Stick with your own kind, Yank. That's what . . .'

'Shut up, laddy,' warned Mr Keaton. 'I've just about had enough of you and your cronies and your endless mouthing of something dirty. Hiding it behind the cloak of patriotism.'

John felt like applauding the games teacher, but he kept quiet, sorting through the bats until he picked up one that felt about right. It had the name 'Louisville Slugger' on the side. The balance was marvellous and he tried a couple of practice swings, sending the bat hissing through the warm afternoon air.

'That's the biggest bat there, John, my man,' said Rick. 'Sure you don't want to try one of the smaller bats?'

'No. This feels fine.'

He tried to stand like the picture he'd seen of the player called Don Mattingly; the bat swung well back until it almost touched his shoulder, holding it near the end of the long, tapered handle, wrists cocked, ready to take the half-step into the swing that Rick had advised.

'Play ball,' called Rick, winding up, the white baseball hidden in the big pitcher's glove. He swung around and his arm whipped forwards.

John didn't see the pitch that well, but he swung, feeling a satisfying jar run up his arms. The ball soared away into the outfield and he dropped the bat, jogging around the bases, waving his arms to the cheers of his mates.

'Jolly well done, John,' complimented Mr Keaton.

'Shot,' grinned Rick.

'Naaw! I reckon 'e give you an easy one,' whined Kenny. 'Wait 'til I get an 'it.'

'Have another go, John,' urged the teacher. 'I still think it was a fluke.'

'Beginner's luck,' said John, smiling.

The second pitch from Rick was faster, and he put a bit of a curve on it. But now John's eye was ready for the pace and movement of the baseball. The bat swung and this time he didn't feel the same shock run to his shoulder. But the ball sailed even further, way over the head of the boy playing out in right field.

'All right, it wasn't a fluke,' called Buster Keaton.

'Felt different, sir,' said John. 'I didn't seem to hit it as hard, but it went miles.'

'Every bat and every ball has what we call a "sweet spot",' said Rick, patting John on the back. 'Guess you got the sweet spot on the Slugger this time.'

'My go, innit!' yelled Kenny Ravven.

'Yes,' said the games master. 'Yes, it's your go.'

Kenny picked up the big bat that John had dropped, giving it a couple of awkward practice swings, holding it more like a cricket bat.

John sat down next to Joe Taylor, watching as the tall American boy wound up, ready to pitch. The arm came slicing round and the ball flashed past Kenny, thwacking into the big glove of the boy playing at catcher.

'Strike one,' said Rick.

'Wasn't ready,' yelled Kenny.

'You ready now?' asked Rick.

'Yeah. Yeah, I am now. But I wasn't.'

'Strike two!' shouted John Greene, as the next ball also whizzed past Kenny's waving bat.

The skinhead said nothing, rubbing his trainers in the dust, as if he didn't quite have the grip he needed.

'Ready?' Kenny didn't reply, merely nodding grimly at the pitcher.

'Strike three! You're out!' Well over half the class joined in the shouting and jeering as Kenny totally missed the ball.

'It was too low! You're tryin' to cheat me you . . . It's not fair.'

'We don't have much time now, Ravven,' called the teacher.

'I want another go! It's not fair. Everyone else got more goes. I can 'it it. Gimme one more ball, Yank! Come on!'

'One more,' nodded Mr Keaton.

Rick winked over at John, wiping sweat from his forehead. He gripped the ball tightly, getting ready to pitch. 'You sure you're ready? Don't want you to complain afterwards.'

The English boy didn't answer. John guessed that his friend was really trying, putting all his effort into the pitch. Kenny nearly got it. The ball just glanced off the top of the bat, angled sideways and hit him in the middle of the face with a sickening crack and a spurt of bright blood.

'D'you see the blood?'

'Thought he'd broken it.'

'So did Kenny.'

The rest of the class, even including the injured skinhead's mates, burst into helpless roars of laughter.

Kenny's first lieutenant, a tall, gangling boy named Bob Jarvis, staggered around, hands clasped to his face, doing a great impression of Ravin' Ravven after the ball hit him.

'Blimey, it's broke! Get the ambulance, me nose is busted!'

Joe Taylor joined in. 'Blood! Look at me 'ands! Blood on 'em. I think . . .' letting his hands droop to his side, falling to the grass, legs kicking up in the air. Finally, with infinite drama, he collapsed into shuddering stillness.

'Almost worth an Oscar, Taylor,' commented Mr Keaton, drily, coming out of the school on to the playing-fields.

'Is Kenneth all right, sir?' asked Rick Okie, worriedly.

'Course he is. Bit of a bruise, that's all. Mr Nolan's taken him along to the hospital for a check-up, but it certainly isn't broken. Maybe it'll knock a bit of sense into him.'

57

'Sorry the baseball game ended like that, sir,' mumbled the American.

'Don't be. It's not as though you deliberately threw the . . . pitch harder than any of the others. Is it? Is it, Rick?'

'Er, well . . . I guess not, sir. Not a *lot* harder than the others.'

There was another great purging gale of laughter. And Mr Keaton joined in it.

So term ended.

Kenny Ravven didn't come back for the last couple of days, choosing to hide his injured nose and his badly-dented pride at home.

John got an invitation from Rick Okie's father to go visit them on the air-base, out north-east of London, and have a look around and maybe even get to play a little real baseball, which was an invitation that John was delighted to receive.

Those couple of moments with the Louisville Slugger swinging in his hands had been real magic. Even better than clouting the ball over the boundary for a six. Better than a good hook-shot in basketball. Now he wanted to try it again.

Rick lent him some copies of American baseball magazines as well as *First Base*, the English magazine. He kept finding references to Don Mattingly, the lefty hitter from the Yankees, who was also one of the finest fielders, at first base, in the game.

John also followed Rick's suggestion that he try and listen to some of the baseball games, broadcast from the States, via the Armed Forces Network on the medium waveband. John managed to find it with a bit of difficulty. Rick's warning about the patchy reception turned out to be right and he kept getting some spillage over the top of the commentary from what he discovered was Radio Two.

But he still heard enough to want to know even more about the game. Towards the end of the first week of the holidays he went up on the Tube with Rick and visited a great bookshop in Charing Cross Road, close by Cambridge Circus. It was called 'Sports Pages' and he found shelves of books about baseball, as well as every other sport he'd ever heard of. He bought a cheap paperback guide to the game and read it through, checking out any questions with Rick.

It was on the Friday night, quite late, when John had the biggest row he'd ever had with his stepfather. And it all began with the baseball game on the music centre.

It was a game between the Yankees, whom he'd sort of adopted as 'his' team, and the Canadian team, the Toronto Blue Jays. The Yankees were leading five runs to three at the top of the fifth innings. Don Mattingly had already batted in two runs, including a towering homer off pitcher Mark Eichorn.

It had rained during the evening and there'd been a crackle of distant thunder, which didn't do much to help the faint, crackly reception of the baseball commentary. Without realizing it, John had gradually been turning up the volume, straining to hear, pressing himself closer to the speakers.

Suddenly the door of his room burst open and his stepfather, face as grim as Arctic ice, came charging in.

'John Elijah Greene!' he roared.

'What?'

'You know very well what?'

'I don't. What's the matter?'

'Don't give me that!'

John was suddenly aware, over the hissing of the radio, that he could hear Norma-Jean crying, and his mother's voice trying to comfort the baby. At the same moment he realized that he'd gradually been turning up the volume, struggling to hear through the crashing surf of static.

'It's a bit loud, isn't it?' he said.

He half-rose as Mike Webber took a step towards him, fist clenching, face tight with anger. 'A *bit* loud? You've got a nerve, John, you really have. You wake up the kid and your mother and me and you don't even say that you're sorry.'

'You goin' to hit me, then?' asked the boy, standing and facing the angry man.

With a visible effort of self-control, his stepfather turned and walked towards the door. He stopped, turning to face him again.

'We can't go on like this, John.'

'What d'you want to do? Throw me out of the flat?'

'Course not. This is your house. It was your home

60

before it was my home.' He sounded weary and John felt his own mixture of fear and anger fading away.

'Look, Mike . . . ,' he began.

'No, John, you look for a change. Sit down a minute. There's things I gotta say. Come on, boy. Sit down on the bed a minute.'

John did as he was told, watching as Mike pushed the door shut and leant against it. He was wearing only a torn T-shirt and pyjama trousers, a silver chain with a St Christopher medal dangled round his neck.

'I'll keep it short, John. Things is bad here and we both know it. If you was older you could move out and find your own place. But you ain't and you can't. Now, there's somethin' in the wind that might change that. We'll know in a few days.'

'What?'

Mike shook his head. 'Can't tell you. Sworn to secrecy. Cut me throat and hope to die.' He tried a smile. 'Anyways, John, it might make everythin' all right for all of us. But I just want you to know that things was over with Kim . . . your mum, and Ben . . . and your father. Long time 'fore I ever showed up. It's true. Ben'll say the same. He an' Kim had just drifted apart. You was too young to notice it, John.'

'Go on.' In the other room his mother had managed to settle Norma-Jean down.

'I love Kim, boy. Really love her. Things aren't great at the moment, but it's hard times. Money's tight. You know that. And me bein' on the dole an' all. But that's behind us. Sun's goin' to shine for us, John. I tell you that.'

'Hope so, Mike.'

'That's all I gotta say. Just that I love Kim and I love Norma-Jean. And if you'd only come part the way to meet me, then I'd love you too, John. Like you was my own son. But you ain't and never will be. Nothin' I can do 'bout that.'

John didn't know what to say. For the first time since the other man had come into their life, he felt a surge of affection for him, seeing the pain that Mike felt about their failed relationship.

'I'm real sorry, Mike,' he managed.

'Yeah,' nodded his stepfather. 'Me too. I'm glad we had a bit of a talk, John. Clear the air a bit. Know what I mean? Anyway, keep the noise down, will you?'

On an impulse the man moved from the door, holding his hand out to the boy. John got up, self-consciously and shook it, feeling oddly grown-up.

After Mike had closed the door and left him alone once more, John sat on the bed and wondered about the strange hints that he'd been given.

'What's goin' on?' he whispered to himself.

On the way to the tube station, John walked past a parked police car, at the kerb, near the end of Hillmarton Road. There were two uniformed men inside it and one of them leaned out of the window and stared at him as he went by. John was used to that kind of attention, but he felt a chill down his back as he thought he recognized the officer as the one who'd chased and nearly caught him a couple of weeks ago.

But nothing was said and he decided he must have been mistaken. In any case, all policemen in uniform looked the same to him.

Rick was waiting at Liverpool Street Station for him, by the main destination board at the end of platform seven.

'Got your ticket?'

'Yeah. Day return to Cambridge. That's where your old man's meetin' us, isn't it?'

'Yeah. Due off in about ten minutes. Looking forward to playing some ball?'

John nodded. 'Bit nervous, playin' with men. I still don't know that much about the game.'

'Doesn't matter. You got what Dad calls good hand-eye co-ordination and good reflexes. You'll be fine, John, fine.'

It was a blazing hot day and at the far end of the platforms, under the long glass roof, they could see a perfect blue sky. John noticed that one of the boards showing where trains were going had suddenly gone haywire. Names of stations and numbers and letters all tumbled ceaselessly over each other like a crazy waterfall of black and white.

A few miles out of London, past a place called Tottenham Hale, John noticed a series of walls on the right side of the line, covered with some of the worst racist graffiti he'd ever seen. He felt himself growing

63

hot with useless anger at the sickness of it all and wondered why nobody bothered to clean it off properly. Some of it looked like it had been there for months, if not years.

He was glad that Rick was looking out of the other side of the carriage and didn't see any of it.

'I love your English countryside,' said the American boy. 'It's so clean and fresh and green and kind of quaint.'

The train was slowing down as it neared some men working on the line. They'd finally passed out beyond the furthest London suburbs into the country, with lakes and narrow rivers. There was a tumbling weir to their right and a camping-field. Both boys leaned out of the window as the Cambridge express crawled over a level-crossing at a village called Roydon.

There was an attractive girl, waiting in the road for the gates to lift. She had a blonde punk haircut. John waved to her and was rewarded with a broad grin and a wave back.

'Reckon she fancies me,' he said to Rick.

'Come on! She's about twenty. Much too old for you, my man. Anyway, it was me she was smiling at.' They both laughed.

Master-Sergeant Richard Okie Senior drove as though the world was about to come to an end. The boys sat in the open back of the pick-up truck, hanging on for dear life as he sped through the winding roads to the American air base.

John was shown round in a lightning tour that left him with only a jumbled impression of large men, laughing a lot, all incredibly busy, in a complex of low buildings and enormous planes. Mum had suggested he take their camera, but Rick had said that wouldn't be a good idea.

They had lunch in a big hall. A burger filled the plate, the meat a full inch thick, with ketchup and a fresh side-salad. Glasses of iced water stood on every table and about fifty different flavours of ice-cream were available.

'You never visited our country, John?' asked a deep-voiced sergeant, who had already told the boy he came from Columbus, Ohio and had three teenage sons.

'No, but I'd like to.'

'I'll give you my address and number, John. Then if you get over Stateside, y'all come see us, you hear me?'

'Thanks,' said John, struggling with culture-shock.

At last it was two o'clock and he followed Rick and the others out to a luxurious changing-room where everyone was getting ready for the baseball. Rick's father had already explained that this was like a practice game, but all of the air-base's best players would be involved. John had already been embarrassed a dozen times by the friendly man's repeated telling of how he'd asked if baseball was called that because it was played at air-bases.

They didn't wear the team's uniforms, everyone

playing in sweat-shirts and either jeans or cut-down shorts. But they had all the finest equipment including, John was pleased to see, several Louisville Slugger bats.

'Richard Junior tells me you're an ace fielder, John,' said Rick Senior.

'I'm all right, I suppose.'

The tall American looked a bit taken aback. 'Is that British understatement John, or does it mean you aren't very good?'

'It's understatement, Dad,' said Rick. He'd gone to get changed and reappeared in electric blue shorts and a T-shirt with the energetic slogan: 'GOGOGOGO' on its front. He was also wearing a baseball cap with the logo of the New York Yankees on it.

'Fine. Then he can start off at left field. Know where that is, John?'

'Yes.'

'Do we have a cap or some shades for John? The sun's damned bright, Richard Junior?'

'I saw an old Padres' cap in the locker-room, Dad.'

'Go get it.'

'That the San Diego Padres?'

The Master-Sergeant nodded. 'Sure is, John.'

Rick's father resembled a technicolour mountain, in a Hawaiian shirt and matching shorts.

The Padres' cap was dark brown with orange letters S and D entwined. John tried it on, feeling a heightening of the buzz of excitement.

'You look good, son,' said Richard Okie Senior.

John hadn't taken any chances. He'd chosen a clean

66

pair of 501s, a dark blue sweat-shirt that didn't fit too tightly, and his most comfortable pair of Adidas trainers.

The match was in a proper kind of stadium, with a grandstand and enormous field, with the bases and pitcher's mound and everything. John felt very nervous as he trotted out towards left field, going even deeper as Rick's father motioned him back. It seemed like the vast, friendly man was in charge of the teams. The glove on John's right hand felt clumsy, but he knew that he'd need it if anyone hit a big line drive in his direction.

He half wanted a chance to show how good he was at fielding and half hoped the ball wouldn't come anywhere near him.

The first batter struck out, missing all three of the legitimate strike pitches. The first pitch to the second man in was a ball, but he swung at the next pitch, steepling it off the face of the bat, sending it soaring high in the hot afternoon sky, towards where John was waiting.

'Catch it, kid!' yelled a fat, scarlet-faced major from the base.

John picked the hit up early, trying to guess where it was going, watching it with all his concentration, but at its highest point it crossed the golden laser of the sun, vanishing. John blinked, eyes watering, trying to see where the baseball had gone.

'Bad luck, son!' called the same plump officer as the ball thudded to the dry turf a yard behind the boy.

Gritting his teeth in disappointment, John turned quickly and picked up the ball, throwing it in all the way to third base. His accuracy got a round of applause from the rest of the fielding side, which made him feel a bit better.

'Here, try these on,' said Rick, running up to him with a pair of the peculiar sun-glasses. They had a flip-down pair of lenses for when you had to look up towards the sun. John took them gratefully and went back to left field to practise using them.

But the ball didn't come his way during the rest of the first innings. The opposition team only managed a single run and then John's side were in to bat.

He was due to go in at five, but the men at bat before him failed to register a score and he was back in the field without touching the bat. During the top of the second innings, he fielded a bouncing ground ball well and helped to put the runner out.

They were still only trailing by the single run when he finally picked up the Slugger, trying a couple of nervous swings as he walked out to the plate. The umpire greeted him with a friendly grin. 'I ain't saying this pitcher's fast, son,' he said, 'but get ready for the scorching smell as the ball passes your eyebrows.'

'I'll watch for it,' said John, trying for a smile and nearly making it.

Nearly.

John was totally boggled by the speed. He'd seen a couple of videos at Rick's flat and watched a game on television, but nothing had prepared him for this. The first ball went by him and he never moved a muscle.

'Strike one,' shouted the umpire.

'Stay loose, kid!' bellowed someone from the players' digout.

At least he tried to swing at the next two pitches but missed them both.

'Strike three an' you're out! Unlucky, boy. Better luck next time.'

John shook his head and dropped the bat, trudging back to join the other members of his team, who all gathered to console him, trying to give him tips on what to do (most of which he immediately forgot).

'Now you've seen him, you can hit him next time up at the bat,' encouraged Rick's dad.

Out in the field, one of the opposition belted a massive hit for a home run, forty feet over John's head. But the next man at bat mis-hit and the ball once more went sailing in the air in his direction.

Remembering what had happened last time, John tried to flip down the dark lenses on the glasses, but in his haste he caught them with the big fielding glove and knocked them to the dirt.

'Not again,' he muttered, determinedly hooking his eyes on to the spinning ball, trying to ignore the sun's brilliant dazzle. He picked out the swirling red pattern of the stitching on the baseball, focusing on that as it fell towards him.

It was going behind him again!

He hardly realized that he'd backed right up against the high wall that marked the edge of the field. The ball was still going behind him, towards the top of the wall where it would register another homer.

'Lift-off,' John said to himself. Half-crouching, then powering himself upwards, glove stretched high above his head, he plucked the ball out of the air and, holding it safely, brought off a great catch.

Encouraged by the reaction to his show in the outfield, John went up to his next turn at the bat in the fourth innings with renewed confidence. His team had drawn level on two runs each.

This time he devoted all of his energy to concentrating on watching the ball from the micro-second that it left the pitcher's hand. This time the speed wasn't so daunting, but the pitch was low and he left it alone hearing the umpire call: 'Ball one!'

The next pitch was slower, curving wickedly, but John braced himself, stepping in to take it early, pulling it hard. He knew from the feel of the impact that he'd found the sweet spot of the bat.

He was so delighted to see the ball go hurtling away between first and second base, skimming towards the wall, that he very nearly forgot to drop the bat and sprint towards first base. He finally reached second base safely.

'Two RBIs,' called Rick, giving him the thumbs-up sign.

'Runs batted in,' said John to himself, delighted with his success. The next batter struck out, but then Rick came in and hit his first pitch into almost exactly the same place as John's hit, sending him sprinting in to complete his own run.

By the end of the sixth innings, the team with John and Rick had a lead of eight to three.

In the final innings, John was on second base, with their last batter at the plate. Master-Sergeant Okie strolled over to the boy, standing near him. Dropping his voice so that the fielding side couldn't hear him, he said, 'You know 'bout stealing a base, son?'

John nodded. 'It's when a runner sprints to the next base, even if the ball hasn't been hit.'

'Or even pitched. Watch the pitcher. Any time you want to risk it, you can go for third base. The catcher'll have the ball and try to run you out there, so the timing's got to be good. But this is the moment to go for it. This way, the guy at bat can just poke it a little way and you should be able to get in to home for the run. Get it, John?'

'Sure.'

'Want me to give you a signal?'

'No. Thanks, but I'd like to try it.'

The pitcher had guessed something was up and he kept glancing over his shoulder at John as he started to wind up. But the boy waited calmly, picking the moment when the ball had just been released.

Heart leaping, John exploded into action, arms pounding, imagining he was Ben Johnson going for the world hundred metres record. There was a yell of warning from the opposition dug-out, but the catcher wasn't quick enough. John sensed the ball being thrown towards the third base and he dived, like he'd seen on the vids, feet first, sliding into the base in a cloud of dust.

'He was out!' shouted the baseman.

'He was in!' countered Rick's father, twice as loudly.

'He was in,' agreed the umpire.

On the next pitch, the man at bat bunted it gently sideways, giving John the chance to dash in for another run.

That was the end of the scoring and John walked off the diamond at the finish of the seventh innings, glowing with the savour of victory, and the knowledge that he'd acquitted himself well.

'Nine to three!' whooped Rick, slapping his friend on the shoulder. 'How 'bout that?' Turning to his father, he added, 'Shame he's not eligible for the base's games, Dad, isn't it?'

For a moment John thought that the man-mountain was going to pick him up and hug him, and he got ready to dodge. But Richard Okie Senior contented himself with a broad grin and a surprisingly gentle pat on the back.

'You done good, boy. Real good. Any time you want to come practise here, just fix it with Richard Junior. For an English kid who never played ball before . . . Wow! You were out of sight, John.'

The rest of the time at the base passed in a haze, with Americans coming up to congratulate him on his debut with them, pressing food and soft drinks on him, until John thought he ran a serious risk of bursting. Rick travelled back with him on the train and they parted at Holborn tube station, Rick going on to change on the Northern Line, John switching to the Piccadilly Line.

'Thanks, Rick,' said John. 'Mean it. Great, just great.'

In bed that night John looked across where a stray shaft of moonlight picked out the dark shape of the San Diego Padres' cap that Rick's father had insisted he keep as a memento. They weren't a team that John knew much about, but he swore that he'd support them as well as Don Mattingly's Yankees.

He slipped quickly into a deep, contented sleep, feeling that things were finally turning out well for him.

8

The uniformed police constable seemed to fill the small living-room, fitting himself between the dining-table and the sideboard. He held his cap in his hands, twisting it round and round. John's mother sat in one of the two faded chintz armchairs and Mike stood in the doorway through to the kitchen. Norma-Jean was sound asleep in her cot on the little rectangle of concrete just outside the back door.

John stood by the dining-table, his school work-folder in front of him. He felt as though he might throw up. Someone had sucked all the air out of the overcrowded room. And he desperately needed to go to the toilet.

'That is your folder, isn't it, John?' asked the policeman.

'Yeah.'

'And that name written on it. Inx, it says. You recognize that?'

The glossy coloured nine by six photo lay alongside the folder. The picture was of the piece that John and his gang had completed on the row of abandoned, tumbledown shops. The piece he'd called 'Jawz' and had enjoyed seeing in the local paper. And had signed with his own artist's tag of 'Inx'.

'The policeman asked if you recognized the name, John,' said Mike, quietly.

'I can see it's the same as on the picture of the big fish,' said the boy, desperately stalling to try and buy some magical thinking time.

'Don't try it on, lad. It's gone six o'clock. I've had a hard, hot shift and I'd really like to get back to the station and file my report and then go home. Come on.'

'Maybe someone else put that on me folder. They could've, couldn't they?'

The policeman nodded, tiredly. 'Yeah, John, they could have.' He pulled out his notebook. 'You got a teacher called Mr Tynan?'

John looked down at the floor, pretending he didn't quite understand the question, feeling even more desperate to go to the toilet.

'Course he does,' interrupted his mother. 'Mr Tynan takes him for art. Gives him good marks. Says he got a real talent.'

'Yes. That's what he told me when I got in touch with him, Mrs Greene.'

'It's Mrs Webber, constable. I got married again to . . .' pointing to Mike.

'Sorry. Anyway, Mr Tynan confirmed that John Elijah Greene is one of his most promising pupils. He hadn't seen your great white shark, John. When I showed it him he didn't have any doubt who'd done it, and he also recognized the signature there, at the bottom. Inx. Like someone might have put on your folder, lad.'

75

Mike straightened from the doorway. 'Listen, I got somethin' to say. You go off and write your report and say what you gotta say. We'll have a good family talk here and then I'll come in with John and see someone down the nick tomorrow morning at ten o'clock. How about that?'

'I don't . . . It's potentially serious, you know. Criminal damage. Rocked some boats round the manor, he has. Personally I don't see much harm, if you stick to rotting heaps that are falling down. But the law's the law, Mr Webber. One or two are shouting for someone to get made a scapegoat.'

'He's not goin' to do a runner, is he? John's a good lad, but he . . . you know. Let us have a talk and come in tomorrow?'

'All right. Ask to see Sergeant Flynn. He'll be on duty. I'll talk to him first. And then we'll see what happens.'

Mike showed the policeman out and John heard the front door of the house shutting. His mother looked up at him, eyes brimming with concern and sadness.

'Gotta go an' have a . . .' he began, when the back door swung open, letting in a flood of hot, dusty air. In walked his father.

'A good, good evening to one and all,' he said. 'I bring . . . What's wrong? Looks like I stepped in on a family funeral.'

Rick was on his own when John reached the flat. After he'd wrapped himself around an ice-cold can of Coke,

John told his friend about the visit from the policeman.

'Didn't know whether to put my hand up for it, or not.'

'Difficult,' agreed the American boy.

'Yeah. Killer, innit? But he'd been to school and got hold of old Tynan. He blew the whistle on me. Still, can't blame him.'

'Then your old man rolled up?'

'Right. He looked like a cat who'd just caught a juicy sparrow. But Mum an' Mike told him about the spray-can pieces and having to go to the nick tomorrow and he got all serious.'

'What was your stepfather like?'

John put the can down on the table, changed his mind and put it on the floor. He rubbed at the small ring of condensation on the table. 'He was real good, Rick. Know what I mean! I thought he'd do a big number about it, but he was all calm and in charge, like.'

'Then they sent you over here and told you to get back by nine?'

'That's right. I don't know . . . don't know what's going on.'

'It'll be OK, John. Can't be that big a deal, what you did. The pieces were really lovely, too. Here, have another drink?'

'Why not?'

John looked at his watch, seeing that it was twenty forty-seven. Less than a quarter of an hour and he

77

ought to be home. Then he'd find out whatever it was that had been so secret for the last week or so.

It was a warm night and as he walked slowly along, from the Caledonian Road, a lot of the large houses had windows open and he could hear the endlessly different kinds of music floating out into the summer darkness. Some reggae came bouncing out, over-topped with classical and what John thought was probably a cello, then a bit of opera, and a fat woman leant out on the sill, singing along with her record. She saw the boy staring up at her and she waved to him, without missing a note. There was the theme music of one of the soaps and then some Indian tune on a sitar.

There was also the smell of cooking. John liked all sorts of food and he could savour them as he strolled towards the traffic lights at the end of the road. There was definitely a curry, but someone in a bed-sit in the same house was frying up sausages and onions. Then John tasted the scent of that Greek thing with aubergines that his mother cooked once, but his father hadn't liked it and she'd never done it again.

John thought that must have been only a short time before his parents had finally split up. He carried that thought with him round the corner into the short expanse of Beacon Hill. He paused once more at the gate, checking his watch: twenty fifty-nine and thirty-seven seconds.

John took several slow, deep breaths, before walking down the side path, round past the dusty conservatory, and in through the back door.

'Hi Mum, hi Dad, hi Mike,' he said.

Ben was sitting at the dining-table, a half-empty glass in front of him and a couple of lager cans at his elbow. Mike sat the other side of the table, looking almost like a mirror image, with the glass and cans arranged in front of him. Mum was in the arm-chair, carefully pouring herself a can of beer, smiling up at John as he came into the flat.

'Want a drink, John?' asked Dad. 'There's another coupla cans in the fridge.'

'No thanks, Dad. Had some Coke over at Rick's.'

'The American boy?'

'Yeah.'

For some reason the words 'American boy' seemed to make the three grown-ups grin at each other. John felt like a newcomer at a party where everyone else has been sharing a private joke – a joke that was about him.

'What's going on?' he asked.

His mother looked at each of her husbands, as if she was waiting for one of them to say something, but wasn't sure which.

'Mike?' she said, after a long pause.

'No, Kim. It's up to Ben.'

'I don't mind if you tell John,' replied the other man.

'No, you tell him, Ben,' urged Kim, sipping at her lager.

'Maybe you ought to tell him, love,' said Ben, still grinning at his son.

'I don't mind who tells me,' said the boy, still standing in the door through to the kitchen. 'Just so's one of you tells me.'

'Shall I tell him, then?' asked Ben. 'That all right with you, Mike? And you, Kim?' They both nodded their agreement.

'Come on Dad?' John said, feeling a prickle of strange excitement.

'Sit down, son. It's like this. We've got a sort of suggestion for you.'

9 Rick punched his right fist hard into his left hand, whooping so loudly that a flock of feeding pigeons rose squawking into the afternoon sunshine, scattering crumbs of bread as they went.

'San Diego! I don't believe it, man. You telling me the truth? That John Elijah Greene of Holloway, London, England is going to go and live in San Diego, California and become a citizen of the United States of America? That's too much, John.'

'I don't believe it myself, Rick. What with gettin' nicked last night and then Dad comin' round and then . . . Pow!' He spread his hands wide to show the extent of the mental explosion.

'I just can't believe it. Dad was posted there once, when he was seconded to the Naval Air Force. There's lotsa airfields round San Diego. Maybe he'll get sent there again one day and we can meet up again. Get slugging together. How 'bout that, John? Sound good to you?'

'Yeah, I reckon so.'

'Blimey, mite,' said the American, adopting a terrible stage Cockney accent. He dropped it just as quickly. 'You don't sound that pleased.'

John sniffed. 'I don't . . . Well, I just sort of don't

know, Rick. It's all so sudden. It won't be like a holiday there. It'll be for ever.'

'Like a life sentence at San Quentin Prison?' grinned Rick.

'No. Not really. Don't be a sap. I mean . . . Dad only heard about this job yesterday, for certain. And he has to fly out in a fortnight. I'll follow him at the end of August. Goodbye home and Mum and . . . everybody and . . .'

'And school and Ravin' Ravven,' said his friend quickly, seeing that John had suddenly got choked up about the enormity of it all.

'Yeah. Yeah, there's that.'

'And goodbye to the police.'

'Right, mate. That Sergeant Flynn wasn't a whole lot of laughs.'

When Ben and Mike took John to the police station, Sergeant Flynn was expecting them. He was a tall man with receding hair and a ferocious ginger moustache that was sprinkled with grey. His eyes were like little blue diamond chips.

'This the lad who likes painting on walls? And you two gentlemen will be . . . ?'

'I'm Ben Greene, Sergeant, and this is John's stepfather, Mike Webber.'

'Right, let's go on through and have a chat. And maybe a cup of tea wouldn't go amiss as well.'

John had heard the expression 'to read someone the riot act', and he knew it meant to really rip someone over doing something wrong.

82

Sergeant Flynn heard Ben and Mike explain about the job in America and how John was to emigrate with his natural father. The policeman listened in silence. Then he read John the riot act.

He told him that if it hadn't been for the news about America then John would have been in juvenile court on Monday morning. And he'd have been charged with criminal damage.

'They were all ruined and falling-down and the pieces we did made them look better and . . .' tried John.

'Your mouth, son,' replied Sergeant Flynn. 'Keep it closed. It doesn't matter in the eyes of the law if the building was built yesterday or a hundred years ago, whether it's crumbling or not. That isn't the point and you'd better realize that, young Master Greene, or you'll run into serious trouble over in the States. And keep out of trouble and away from spray-cans until you fly out.'

'Thanks, Sergeant,' said Ben, standing up and putting his arm around his son's shoulders. 'He won't do it again.'

'He'd better not,' replied the officer, grimly. 'He'd better not.'

'I felt like I was six years old and two feet tall,' said John, finishing telling Rick about the visit to the police station.

'Anyway, that's over. You going to forget about being Inx for a bit? There's some real good street artists over in the States.'

83

'I know. Seen some of their pieces in books. I reckon I'll watch it for a bit.'

'Good thinking, my man. And you go in, what? Around four weeks? Then you'll be in the land of the free and the home of the brave. And the land of Major League Baseball, John.'

'Yeah. I've thought of that as well.'

The days raced by.

Since he was travelling on his own, John had to apply for a passport. He sat in the photo-booth in the post office, waiting for the light to come on, then hung around in the crowd for the strip of four prints of himself. He grinned with embarrassment at the way someone seemed to have poured concrete into the muscles of his face, making each picture look more frozen than the one before.

All his possessions had to be crated up and des-patched to wait for his arrival. Clothes had to be bought to cater for the warmer, sunnier weather of Southern California. When he'd looked up the city on his school atlas, John had been surprised to find that it was down the coast from Los Angeles and only a few miles from a town called Tijuana that marked the border with Mexico.

His father went off at a tearful party, with distant cousins and aunts and uncles, whom John had never seen, filling the Beacon Hill flat to overflowing. A phone call a couple of days later told John about the apartment his father had found, helped by the engin-eering firm who'd hired him. John would have his own room, and it was only two or three miles from the Pacific Ocean.

As the summer days ran by, John began to experience a strange feeling of unreality. With less than a week left, he started thinking that it was the last time he'd visit the local cinema, or go to the supermarket for his mother, or walk past his old school or . . . So many last times.

His relationship with Mike, with all the tension finally gone, became calm and friendly. His step-father took him on shopping expeditions, trying to persuade him to buy a pair of mirrored sun-glasses and a peaked denim cap. He laughed at John's protest that it would make him look like some sixties hippy.

Rick had to go back to the base at Suffolk only a couple of days before John was due to fly out from Heathrow. The two boys walked together along the evening streets of North London, easy in each other's company, both of them aware that this might be their last ever meeting.

'Write me, John.'

'Sure. And you write to me an' all, Rick.'

'You got it.'

Too soon it was time for Rick to catch a bus back to rejoin his father and there was a moment between them when neither boy knew what to say.

'Well, this is it, mate,' said John, seeing the looming shape of the red bus appearing round the corner.

'Right. Thanks for helping me out at school, John. Wish I could be there in San Diego to do the same for you. But you'll be fine.'

'Hope so. Take care, Rick. See you, one day.'

There was time for a tentative shake of the hand and then Rick was on the platform. Just as the bus began to pull away, he shouted out to the English boy.

'Keep swinging, John. See you in the Majors.'

There was a gust of wind in the street that blew clouds of gritty dust around. It dashed into John's face and made his eyes water.

On the last evening, Mum was preparing a special farewell supper of John's favourite food: a steaming plate brimming with homemade lasagna, followed by Kim's real speciality, a chocolate mousse with tiny chips of grated mint and orange chocolate scattered over it.

She'd told him he had to get to bed early and then shooed him out of the house so she could get on with the cooking.

'Come back at eight, sharp, on the dot.'

It left John about an hour and a half for a positively last walk around the neighbourhood.

He saw Joe Taylor with Shane Harvey and three or four other friends, two of them with shoulder-bags that he knew held cans of spray-paint, off to do a piece somewhere. They spotted him and all waved, vanishing down a cross-street.

It gave him a pang to realize that life was going on without him, and would always go on without him. For a moment, John felt what it must be like to be a ghost.

He felt at a loose end, like an accident waiting to

happen. He'd said his goodbyes to everyone and visited all his favourite places. By this time tomorrow he'd be well on his way, somewhere over the ice of northern America, winging south towards California.

He scuffed his feet on the pavement, moving out of the way as a pair of elderly women bustled by him, arguing noisily about the price of wiping-up cloths. A dog was barking in a front garden, leaping up and down so that its sharp face kept appearing and then disappearing. As always, there was music. The Los Lobos version of 'La Bamba' that had been a hit a couple of years back was playing from an upper window of a crumbling semi-detached house. Overlaid with dust, there was the late summer scent of a rosebush in a front patio, the sharp tang of petrol from a building next door where a couple of Indian boys were working on a stripped-down motor-cycle.

Off to the left John could see, along a narrow alley, the doors of some garages, several of them decorated with some of his early pieces.

On an impulse he walked down the lane, off the main road, interested to see how the spray-can pictures had survived. It was at least a year since he'd done them and he wondered if the colours had faded at all. To his disappointment he saw that younger kids had scrawled all over his carefully planned pieces, obscuring them under messy webs of black.

Only in one corner of one of the doors could he still see the remains of one of the works, with his tag, Inx, in maroon and silver.

★

It took a real effort for him to force down the monstrous portions of lasagna and chocolate mousse that Mum served up. But he knew how much trouble she'd gone to and how upset she'd be if he didn't do the last supper justice.

He was too excited and too sad to enjoy the food. It truly was his last night in England. Mike had bought a bottle of champagne. Well, it was *nearly* champagne, he said and it bubbled and tasted nice. Mum kept on having a bit of a weep, and John kept telling her he was only going to America. Not like going to the moon, he said.

Without any of them really noticing it, the clock teased its way round to eleven o'clock.

'Goodness, Johnny boy!' exclaimed Mum. 'Time for bed. Big day tomorrow.'

He stood up, feeling a bit wobbly at the knees. 'Right, Mum. Thanks for the meal and everything and thanks for the champagne, Mike. Really nice. G'night, both of you.'

'G'night, son,' said his stepfather.

'Night, John,' said his mother, her voice trembling. She sniffed and reached for a hanky.

On an impulse, he decided to wear his battered San Diego Padres' baseball cap for the journey, jamming it on his head at a jaunty angle. His father was going to meet him off the plane at LA airport and they'd then take the shuttle together to San Diego.

John paused in the door of his room, looking at it, seeing it tidier and emptier than it had ever been. The bed was neatly made, the cupboards closed. Nothing of his remained. Like it was waiting for a new tenant.

The hand on his shoulder made him jump. It was Mike. 'Just wanted to say, son, that this room'll always be here for you. Whatever happens. Just . . . well . . . you know.'

The jumbo jet levelled off and the air-hostess, knowing the young black teenager was flying alone, came and asked him if he wanted something.

More than anything in the entire world at that moment, John wanted his Mum to cuddle him and take away the sadness. But he couldn't say that.

'I'd really like a Coke, please,' he said.

10 Four days into September and the weather in San Diego was staggeringly beautiful; mild sunny days under cloudless skies and not a hint of rain. John's father had bought a second-hand green Volkswagen and he took his son on several tours of the city and the surrounding countryside.

The flight was fine and they'd finally arrived at the apartment close to midnight. John had been utterly exhausted and went straight to bed. Now, after nearly a week, the jet-lag was wearing off, but culture-shock still kept gripping him by the throat. It was partly the sensation of walking around in a permanent TV setting. Everything looked like it had come out of the A-Team or Miami Vice or Dynasty.

John's first desire was to learn a bit about the city before he started at the local Junior High School. That way, he guessed it might be easier to get integrated rather than starting cold.

At least he had the Padres' cap.

He was wearing it as he lay on his bed and flipped again through the guide book that Dad had bought for him.

One thing that he hadn't known was that the history of California really began in San Diego. A Portuguese captain called Juan Rodriguez Cabrillo had landed there right back in 1542. Sixty years later it provided a harbour for the laden Spanish galleons. In 1796 a priest called Father Serra built a mission in the growing settlement. Now, San Diego was the second largest city in the whole state.

Ben Greene had also taken John on a site-seeing cruise along the coast, giving him a wonderful view of the spectacular scenery. They visited Balboa Park, which was the largest of its kind in the whole United States. They spent all day there and left feeling that they'd hardly scratched the surface of the place. There was a wonderful zoo, although John had private doubts about the morality of keeping animals in cages, and half a dozen museums, all set in acres of greenery.

The Greene's apartment was in a quiet side road to the north-east of the city, only a mile or so from the centre. The street map was quite complicated and John asked Dad if he could buy a bike to go and explore it.

'Not yet. Get a mate . . . buddy . . . to show you round, son. San Diego might look a bit like the Garden of Eden when you compare it to Holloway, but it's got its own kind of snakes. So you be careful.'

One mistake that John's dad was able to correct for his son was over the pronunciation of names. There was a district marked on the map, called 'La Jolla', which John read out like it was spelled.

Dad laughed. 'I made that one, too. It's Spanish for jewel and it's pronounced "La Hoya". Tricky, ain't it?'

*

The building where they lived had a really high number. Walking around, John had already noticed streets with numbers going up past four thousand. Dad told him that in Los Angeles they went up over ten thousand, because some of the major residential streets wound in and out for miles and miles.

It was white stucco with an entrance porch and security locks and entry-phones for visitors. There were eight apartments in the block and they rented the one on the first floor at the back, overlooking a shady garden. Dad also pointed out that the Americans called the first floor the second floor and the ground floor the first floor, which was yet another thing for John to try and remember.

They had a narrow hall, leading into a living-room that was long and cool with colour telly, sofa and three saggy armchairs. The kitchen opened off it, with electric stove, fridge, washing-machine and freezer. The two bedrooms and bathroom were off to the left of the living-room.

John's personal things had arrived safely from the shippers and his father had unpacked the crates, but left the boy to put everything away where he wanted it to go. With his music centre, adapted for the different American electricity, and his albums, John was able to lie on his bed and close his eyes and imagine that he was back in England. Oddly, he hadn't yet felt very homesick. There just hadn't been the time.

One thing that they had in the apartment was air-conditioning. It worked like a heater in reverse, blowing cool, refrigerated air through the rooms, battling against the late summer heat of the West Coast.

The other thing that San Diego had was its own baseball team, the Padres, whose stadium was almost within walking distance of John's new home. John had checked out their records in some of the books and magazines owned by Rick's father, and they made fairly disappointing reading. During the seventies the Padres had one of the worst records in the National League, or any other league, come to that. But in the last five or six years, things had begun to improve and they'd actually won more games than they lost in some seasons.

Their pitching was a weakness, but they had a good outfielder, number 19, Tony Gwynn. A left-handed batter, like John, he'd featured in several of the League's best batting performances, making over a hundred runs in a season and leading with over two hundred hits.

'Any chance of getting to see a baseball game, Dad?' John had asked. He'd waited before bothering his father with it, waited all of a minute and a quarter after they met up at the space-age airport in Los Angeles.

The firm that had hired John's father employed a lot of men locally. When his boss heard that Ben Greene's son was heading out to San Diego to live, he immediately arranged for the boy to be included in a party of a dozen teenagers going to see the game between the local Padres and the visiting Cincinnati Reds.

The idea of mingling with the local boys made John feel really nervous. It wasn't like going up to watch Spurs with a few mates, or even going up to the air-base with Rick.

'One of them's coming round this evening to meet up and have a chat 'bout the school and the ball game an' all that,' said Dad. 'Name's Merle Huston. His father's in charge of my section at work. Nice kid. Could do with a hair-cut in my opinion.' Ben Greene laughed. 'But he's still a nice kid. You'll like him, John.'

John wasn't so sure of that.

Merle Huston had the longest hair of any boy that John had ever seen. It was a lightish brown colour, bleached lighter in places by the Californian sun, hanging dead straight to within a half inch of his broad leather belt. He wore stone-washed jeans and a skinny tank-top, torn around the armpits. His eyes were blue and clear and he wore a glittering metal brace, wired around top and bottom teeth.

Ben Greene introduced the two boys, then left them together in the living-room, explaining that he had to go and get some food at the late-night delicatessen a few blocks away. John figured that his father had deliberately invented the errand to leave them on their own, so they'd feel easier.

He didn't feel easier.

'How long you been in San Diego?'

'Only a week or so. Still not used to it at all, you know.'

'Like it?'

'Think so. Weather's great.'

Merle nodded. 'Heard the weather's real deathly in England. Rains all the time. My gramps was there in the war.'

John felt, oddly, that he should defend the climate of the old country. 'It's not that bad all of the time. Honest.'

'Some of the time, not all of the time,' grinned Merle, speaking as if he was quoting from a song.

'Right,' agreed John, also grinning. 'Want a Coke, Merle?'

'No, thanks. Got any designer water? Perrier, something like that?'

'Tap water?'

'No thanks. I don't drink tap water.'

'Why not?'

Merle grinned. 'Fishes pee in it, John.'

The English boy grinned back. Already he was feeling easier.

The big Jack Murphy stadium in San Diego was crowded with people. The fans seemed to mingle in a friendly way, with some competitive taunting, mainly centred on the traditionally poor record of the Padres. The programme that Merle insisted on buying for John was full of pictures and players' profiles and reams of statistics. They bought burgers and cartons of soft drinks, iced, with big bags of fresh popcorn.

'Seats are up here, John,' said Merle. 'Rest of my gang are probably here already. Yeah, there they are!' He waved a hand.

John felt a flutter of nerves again, but the warmth of the welcome washed it away in seconds. He was glad that he'd worn the Padres cap, and glad too that it didn't look new, like he'd just gone out and bought it. To the half dozen San Diego kids it acted like a passport.

All the gang were between twelve and fourteen. Two were black and one Chinese. To John's surprise, one was female.

Their seats were around thirty rows back, overlooking first base. The popcorn was handed around and everyone discussed the starting line-ups of the two teams. John had read up on the Padres and he was able to keep up his end of the discussion, which amazed the local teenagers.

'How come you know so much, John?' asked the girl, whose name was Krysty King.

'Read some. Seen some on telly back home. Got an American friend who taught me some.'

'You supported the Padres?' asked a chubby black boy, whose name John hadn't caught.

The note of disbelief was clear. John was tempted to lie, but he decided the truth was probably a little better. 'No. Not until I knew Dad was coming out here. I supported the Yankees.'

'You have a favourite player, John?' asked Merle, passing round the popcorn.

'Don Mattingly.' There was a chorus of agreement

and nods from the group around him. 'He's a lefty like me.'

'You play, John?' asked someone. John didn't see who it was.

'Kind of. Only a bit though,' he added hastily, seeing he was in danger of digging a trap for himself. 'Once or twice, that's all.'

'What d'you play, John?' called Krysty.

'Short-stop and I bat four.'

'A left slugger who plays short-stop,' said Merle Huston, wonderingly. 'You are a gift from the angels, my man.'

'Why?'

'We play for a team here,' explained the fair-haired boy. 'And our short-stop quit the game to take up some serious skateboarding. He was a lefty as well. So . . .'

The black boy in the next seat laughed. 'Eugene might have been a lefty, Merle, but he wasn't no slugger for us.'

'Not batting less than one hundred, he wasn't. No way.'

They all joined in the laughter. John rubbed the side of his nose where he was afraid a zit was beginning to sprout. 'Look, I'm not . . . I mean, I haven't played much and . . .'

Merle patted him on the arm. 'Relax, John. Don't matter how bad you are, you got to be better than Eugene. Truly.'

Krysty smiled at the English newcomer. 'He's right, John. Ronald Macdonald's better than Eugene.'

'Donald Duck was better.'

'Wiley Coyote was better.'

Merle topped them all. 'Ronald Reagan was a better hitter than Eugene!'

John's excitement bubbled up as the teams took the field. The diamond was clearly marked, the bases a startling white. As far as he could see, the big Jack Murphy Stadium was nearly full to its fifty thousand capacity. From the home base to the furthest wall, out in far centrefield, was just over four hundred feet.

The top of the first inning saw the Cincinnati Reds batting. They were wearing their road uniform of grey shirts with the name 'Cincinati' in large red capitals across the chest. The starting pitcher for the Padres began badly, giving up a grand slam homer to Eric Davis, who brought home all the three men out on the bases with a massive drive over the wall.

Two more runs were batted in by the Reds in their second innings when Davis hit a double.

To the disappointment of John and the rest of the loyal Padres fans, the Cincinati pitcher shut the San Diego hitters out for the first two innings, leaving the score at the top of the third at a depressing six to zero for the visitor.

'They're goin' to bring in Goose Gossage,' yelled Krysty, spotting the Padres' relief pitcher warming.

The number Fifty-Four looked quite old to John, though he knew that some baseball players kept going well past their fortieth birthdays.

Rich Gossage struck out three of the Reds' top men

in succession in the third inning to spark a San Diego revival. In the third and fourth innings the Padres slotted away an amazing seven runs. Outfielder Tony Gwynn hit a great two run homer as well as a single. Stan Jefferson, their lead-off man at the bat, also chipped in with a home run that screamed long and low, just carrying clear of the wall.

The group of John's new friends went wild, all leaping up and down, popcorn flying everywhere, cheering and slapping each other's hands. John found himself joining in the enthusiasm, though in England he'd have found it all a bit embarrassing.

The next four innings were fairly uneventful for both teams. Rich Gossage managed to hold the Reds to only a single run, making the scores level at seven runs apiece.

The top of the eighth brought another home run, bringing in a second man off first base, taking the Cincinnati Reds to a lead of nine to seven. Despite coming close, having the bases loaded with three men at one point, the San Diego Padres just couldn't score, incurring the disgust of Merle Huston.

'Darn it! The old story of these guys. So close and yet so darned far. Thought you might have brought the Padres some luck, John. Guess I was too hopeful for them.'

Gossage held the visitors during the top of the ninth and final inning, leaving the Padres just those elusive two runs behind.

Jefferson slugged a triple, bringing himself all the way round to third base. Some wild and nervous

99

pitching brought a walk to the next man at bat, allowing Jefferson in to score a run.

'Just one in it,' said John, excitedly.

A few minutes later in the same innings and the Padres had managed to get a man safe at first base, but they also had two batters out. One more and the game was over and lost. But the tying run was aboard and the possible winning hit coming up at the plate. One of the great things John liked about baseball was that a game was never lost until it was over.

Gwynn came up to bat, swinging, looking the coolest person in the stadium. The first pitch was low and to the left. Ball one. The second was a fast ball that whistled through to the catcher. One and one. Next came a viciously dipping curve ball that Gwynn swung at and missed, hearing it thwack into the massive glove of the catcher. Two strikes and one ball. One more strike against the hitter and the game was done.

John sat on the edge of his seat, nails dug into the palms of his hands with the tension. Merle was jigging from side to side and Krysty was biting her nails clear up to the knuckles.

The fourth pitch was another fast ball, rifle-straight. Gwynn swung and hit it with the distinctive sound of a big strike. The white ball rocketed up and up, away and away, over the heads of the outfield, way over the wall for a huge home run, bringing in the player off first base.

Which gave victory to the San Diego Padres by the narrow margin of ten runs to nine.

'You *were* lucky!!' yelled Merle to John, pumping his hand.

On the way to the apartment, John couldn't stop talking about the game. The evening air of the Pacific was warm and scented with flowers, as he and Merle Huston strolled back through the city.

'You wanna come try out with us?' asked the American boy. 'Day after tomorrow?'

'Like to Merle, but . . .'

'You can throw a ball inside a barn and hit a wall? Then you're better than Eugene. Come and try. I'll call for you.'

They were outside the front of the house. Merle turned after saying goodbye, then hesitated. 'Hey, John?'

'Yeah?'

'School's back next week.'

'I know. I wondered if we'd be in the same class or anything?'

'Could be. But I was thinking . . . There's a kind of tradition in the gang that we go to the zoo in the last week of the summer vacation. We're going tomorrow. Want to come?'

John grinned. 'Love to. Dad says it's one of the best zoos in the world.'

'It is. And there's kinda heaps to do in Balboa Park.'

'Thanks.'

'Call for you at nine.'

'It's a date, mate,' said John.

'Right here, tomorrow?'

'Sure. At home.'

It was only when John was getting ready for bed, after telling his father all about the baseball game, that he realized what he'd said about the San Diego apartment.

He'd called it 'home'

Home.

11 John quickly realized that his previous visit to Balboa Park, with his father, had only scratched the surface of the place. They'd spent nearly an entire day there just after John arrived in San Diego, but seeing it with Merle Huston and the other members of their gang gave him an insight into the hugeness of the space.

As they walked and ran and joked around the Park, John tried to hang on to some of his impressions, ready for his promised letter back to England to Mum and Mike.

'Not like an ordinary sort of zoo. There's thousands of birds and animals and all that but they aren't in cages. There're open kind of enclosures and they live in something close to their natural habitat. (That's what the guide book said.) You can't believe how great the weather is. And there's a place like a planetarium that takes you on a trip out into the stars. Real lift-off sort of feeling.'

As at the baseball game, John was surprised how relaxed he felt with the other teenagers. When they split into smaller groups and then mingled and split again, he found himself generally in a foursome with Merle Huston, Krysty King and the chubby black boy, whose name he now knew was Henry Wexner.

Everyone called him Hank and he played catcher in their team.

After the zoo they walked along to the Hall of Champions, where some of the more famous sportsmen and women from San Diego were honoured. Hank was quick to drag John along to show him Ted Williams, one of the all-time greatest hitters in baseball history.

John read out the details in an awed voice. 'Lifetime record of two thousand six hundred and fifty-four hits. Five hundred and twenty-one home runs. Lifetime average of three forty-four. Last man to bat over four hundred in a season. American League batting champion six times! Wow! Hall of Famer in nineteen sixty-six.'

Merle grinned. 'If you wanna know about hitting you ought to read his book on it. The best, John, I tell you. And he was a lefty like you.'

Which reminded John that tomorrow he was going to have to go out with his new friends and expose his innocence in actually playing ball. He wondered how long they'd stay his friends if he flunked out on it. Maybe he'd be worse than Eugene!

'Time for food, John. You like Mexican?'

'Mum used to buy those takeaway crispy things sometimes.'

Krysty nodded. 'Being so close to Tijuana and the border there's loads of cheap burrito joints around town. We'll go to Manuels.'

On the way they walked past the side of a large

tenement building and John was amazed to see four teenagers working openly on it with a range of spray-cans and even an airbrush with a battery-powered motor, decorating the wall with a fabulous piece of street art. Even from his short time in the city he recognized that it was like a mural of all aspects of life in San Diego. Boats in the harbour jostled with the animals in the zoo, street scenes and automobiles, and near the top right one boy was working on a more-than-lifesize baseball player.

'That's Tony Gwynn,' he said, spotting the number 19 on the player's shirt. 'That's a terrific piece they're doin' there.'

Hank Wexner stood by the English boy, looking up at the wall. 'You like it, John?'

'Yeah. It's great. In England you'd get busted for tryin' something like that.'

'Really?' exclaimed Merle. 'This is a city-sponsored scheme. Only the best artists get to work on stuff like that. Hank's big brother, Rafe, is one of them.'

'You done that kind of thing, John?' asked Hank, interestedly.

'Yeah. *And* I got busted. I'd love the chance to work on something serious like that. It's . . . it's just . . . Really wicked!'

Manuel's Border Eatery was an interesting experience for John.

'I couldn't believe how many different kinds of stuff there was in Mexican food,' he wrote. 'Fortunately all my mates know a lot about it so everyone got different

105

things and sort of shared them out so I got to try lots of different things and find out which ones I liked. Mostly they were different kinds of pancake things with hundreds of different (got to stop using different all the time! Think what old Piggy Blount would say!). Did you, get the card saying I got here all right? Oh, yeah, I was saying about Mexican food. You can have these pancakes folded or flat or crisp or soggy or cooked with a filling in or with a cooked filling stuck in or a salad and stuff. I think it's quite healthy. Dad says it's good for me. They call them different (sorry) names like tacos and burros and enchiladas and tortillas and tostadas and burritos. And I tried bits of them all and they was all really dead delicious. But dead hot as well. Lots of chilly peppers. Not sure if that's how you spell it. Girl called Krysty wrote all the names of the pancakes out for me.'

John had been very relieved that there were glasses of iced water available at their tables in the pavement restaurant. The only thing that surprised him was that no steam came hissing out of his mouth as he drank after gulping great bits from the hot, spiced pancakes that everyone was tucking into. There was a certain satisfaction in seeing that Hank's eyes were watering as much as his from the meal.

'I'm glad you're settlin' down all right here, son,' said his father, as they sat watching television together that evening. 'I know what a big uprooting it's been for you. Friends, home an' all, to travel half-way round the world to live with your old father. Know it's not easy.'

'I like it here, Dad. Honest and true. I like the apartment, and the kids round here are dead friendly. Bit worried 'bout playin' baseball tomorrow, in case I make a right fool of meself.'

Ben Greene smiled across at his son. 'You'll do fine. Listen, I'll just drop a line to put in with your letter and you can go post it.'

'Sure thing.'

John happened to walk past the table where his father was writing the note, and he saw the first attempt. It finished up, to Mum, saying: 'It's good, Kim. Wish you were here.'

The final draft of the note, when John saw it, omitted those last four words.

The act of sending a letter back to England, to his mother, brought the first wave of homesickness that John had experienced. Lying in his bed, the air-conditioning humming and chirping away outside the window, he was conscious of being an alien. There'd been a science fiction novel that he'd once read, called *Stranger in a Strange Land*. And that was how he felt. What was John Elijah Greene from Holloway, aged thirteen, doing trying to get to sleep in San Diego, California? Maybe he should have stayed in England and tried to get on better with his stepfather?

He woke up sweating, checking the time. It was ten past two in the morning. He could just catch the occasional sound of traffic on the main highway a few blocks away.

It had been a bad dream.

He'd been in England, but it had American weather; a scorching sun that bounced off a huge expanse of white concrete wall, hundreds of yards long, and at least twenty feet high. He was supposed to work out a piece on it, which involved a complicated pattern centring on his tag of Inx, but all he had was a single battered aerosol can of very light cream paint that hardly marked the wall at all. Far away, walking slowly and inexorably towards him, John could make out the uniformed shape of a policeman, rapping on the stone with his truncheon.

Only it wasn't a truncheon. It was a tapering baseball bat.

The spray-can was running out, spluttering feebly, dribbling down his sleeve. Mum was there in the dream, holding baby Norma-Jean, and they were both smiling all the time.

The policeman was drawing closer and closer, the bat striking the wall with an echoing, remorseless sound. Then John heard the voice, seeming as if it actually came from behind the wall. It kept repeating, over and over, higher and higher: 'Hit your homer at home hit your homer at home hit your homer at home hit . . .'

Which was when he woke up.

The boy didn't want to disturb his father so he pulled on his tracksuit trousers and padded, bare-footed into the neat kitchen. He opened the fridge and poured himself a glass of cold orange juice.

108

Back in the living-room, for something to do to try and calm himself down a bit, John turned on the television, making sure the sound was switched as low as it would go. It was an old film about the American Civil War. He'd seen it before, because it had been one of his grandma's favourites and they'd had it on video. It was called *Gone With The Wind*.

He sat on the sofa, nursing the glass, seeing that the film had run near its end.

The main character, played by an English actress, brought the climax with the words: 'Tomorrow is another day'.

John thought that might be a good time to go back to bed.

12

'Today's the day you go and have a knock-around with your mates, innit, John?' asked his father.

'Yeah. This afternoon.'

'You sound like someone goin' to their own hanging, son. Thought you liked baseball.'

'I do, Dad. Like it a lot. Reckon I could even be quite good. But I'm worried in front of . . . You know. They'll all have their own gear and everything and know each other. When it's a friend you know well, you put up with a lot more than from some kid you've hardly met.'

Ben Greene was heating some potato waffles under the grill, strips of lean bacon spitting and crackling in the pan. Fresh coffee was bubbling in the electric percolator and two slices of wholewheat toast popped up, perfectly toasted. Sunshine came lancing through the slats of the blind, boasting of another wonderful San Diego morning.

'Know what you mean, John. Go and sit down and watch the telly. See if there's anythin' on "Good Morning, America" today. I'll bring the food in.'

John had watched the news programme on breakfast telly most days since he'd arrived, and he'd yet to see a single item about England. It was like his past had disappeared, vanished like a ship sailing into the Bermuda Triangle. This time there was an item about zoning houses and another on beach pollution somewhere up the coast.

'We'll take a break right now and come back to our guest, Herbie Anschlevicz, the hypnotizing vet, as well as the latest Hollywood tittle-tattle. And in the news we have more worries in the Gulf, a heightening of tension in the transport dispute and a look at what's happening back in Merry Olde England. Right after the break.'

A bronzed man with face-lifted eyes appeared, singing the praises of his used car business and John called for his father. 'Something about England, Dad! On the news.'

Ben came in, balancing two plates of food on a pale blue plastic tray, with two large mugs of coffee. He put it down carefully and joined John on the sofa to watch.

The item came at the very end of the news, after a piece on a woman in Lemon Grove, a part of the city, whose pet poodle had learned to ride a surfboard up and down her pool.

'Hey, it's going to be somethin' real important,' laughed Dad.

'You may have wondered what Margaret Thatcher's fire-fighters get up to when they aren't battling jolly old blazes, don't you know.' It was delivered in an excruciating parody of an English accent.

John and his father watched on, unable to believe what they were seeing. After nothing at all about the old country, there was this! Some firemen down in the West Country had built a fibreglass model of the Loch Ness Monster and were going to take it and sail along the loch for charity.

The film lasted about ninety seconds. And that was that.

Ben and his son hooted with laughter. 'Government might have fallen, earthquakes in Manchester and we'd know nothing,' grinned the man. 'But we know about a plastic Nessie!'

'Did you notice it was raining, Dad?' asked John.

The mailman delivered a letter that morning, addressed to John E. Greene. The return address was Beacon Hill, Holloway, London.

'Goin' in my room to play some music, Dad,' he said.

'Sure. Let me know if Mum says anything I ought to know.'

John put on a Billie Holiday album, finding the first track was the slow, sad song of nostalgia, 'As Time Goes By'. But he let it play, sitting on the bed and unfolding the thin, crinkly blue paper. He recognized his mother's rounded writing.

The letter had come immediately she'd got his first card, telling of the safe arrival, but obviously before she'd got any letters.

'Dearest son, I was glad to get the card and know you'd made it across the sea. From the letter I got from your father it sounds like San Diego is a nice place and with more sun than we get here. As usual,

112

the summer's rotten. Mike's job is going well. Norma-Jean misses you and won't sleep at night. I miss you and you know that Mike does too in his way.

'The policeman come round the other night to ask after you. I said it was nice but Mike said it was just because he wanted to make sure you'd really gone. I don't know about that. No news from the family. Except your Aunty Enid has to go into hospital for a minor op. Saw Joe Taylor and the Harvey twins yesterday down Camden Town. They both said for me to wish you luck over there. That's all. Hope it won't be too long before you come visit us, or if God's kind we might come to California one day. The flat's very quiet and empty without you, John. Give Ben my love and tell him . . .' Then something was crossed out. 'Lots of love, John. From all of us, Mum.'

A careful application of cold water around the eyes removed most of the signs that John had been upset by his mother's letter. It had somehow brought to him the realization of how far he'd come. He remembered an English saying about burning your bridges behind you. He hadn't exactly done that, because he could go back to England if he really wanted to. But that was unimaginable. Having got here . . . then to trail back.

'No,' he said, to himself.

Dad was still in the living-room, watching the television. His job didn't start until eleven that day. There was an anti-drug advert on as John walked in. 'Is it worth letting your lungs go to pot? No, it's not.

You guys remember that you can't fly when you're high.'

'Hear that, son,' said Ben Greene.

'I'm not that stupid, Dad.'

'Good. Anythin' in your mum's letter?'

'Not really. Here, you can read it.'

His father took the airmail letter and went into his own bedroom with it, closing the door behind him. A few minutes later John heard him go into the bathroom and the sound of running water. When he finally came back into the living-room John saw that his father had washed his face and shaved. Neither of them said anything about the letter.

'What time's baseball?'

'Merle's callin' for me around one.'

'Then we ought to go and do our shopping now, hadn't we?'

'What shopping?'

Dad put his arm around his son's shoulders, smiling broadly. 'Wait an' see, John. Just you wait an' see.'

It was one of the best sports shops that John had ever seen. Dad led the way up to the baseball department, past rows of sweat-shirts and caps. A tanned young man came and asked if he could help.

'My son's got a baseball practice this afternoon. I want him to have a bat.'

'Oh, Dad! That's real . . . thanks.'

'What kind, young man? And what weight? What

finish? Thirty-two ounce from your height and build. Aluminium or wood?'

'Wood, please. Have you got any Louisville Sluggers? I like them.'

The assistant grinned. 'Have we? Does a bear . . . Pardon me. We do. We got bats made from the finest white ash from the Adirondack range of mountains. Clear or natural or flame-treated finish. You want it, we got it. Let's go look.'

In the end, after trying several practice swings, John picked a bat very much like the one he'd used at the American Air Force Base, which seemed like years ago.

'Anything else?'

Ben looked at his son. 'Can't afford the full uniform yet, John. But, if there's one other thing you really need?'

John bit his lip. He knew that he desperately wanted a fielding glove.

'Where d'you field?' asked the assistant. 'You look like an infielder to me?'

'Short-stop.'

'For sure. Here, look at these gloves.'

John noticed his father craning his neck to try and read the price ticket. The laced glove had four separate fingers and a thumb and was comparatively small; only about nine inches from tip to the heel. He tried one on and found it a loose fit.

'That's how it has to be,' he explained to his father. 'Got a loop inside it so you can get a good grip. It's terrific, Dad. Can I have . . . Can we afford it?'

'Go an' have a look at them football shirts?' replied Ben. 'And I'll sort out whether we can afford it.'

As they drove back to the apartment, all the windows open in the Volkswagen, relishing the sea breeze, John cradled the bat, the glove already on his right hand. The assistant had checked he was a lefty before selling the fielding glove.

'All you got to do now, is go and do your best, John,' said Dad. 'That's all either of us can do, out here. You an' me, son. We both do our best, then we'll make it.'

'I know, Dad.'

'Just wanted to tell you how much it means havin' you with me. Know what I mean?'

John simply nodded.

The game took place in a local park, only a mile from the apartment. Merle arrived and the two boys walked together. John, carrying his new glove and bat, feeling absurdly self-conscious.

'It won't be like a serious game. Just to give everyone a chance to try out ready for when we get back to school. A lot of us are in the squad there as well as our own team.'

Once they reached the park, John couldn't wait to get started.

All the gang that he'd met before were there, plus another dozen or more. Five of them were girls. Merle was in charge and he introduced John to everyone there, and then began the process of picking a couple

116

of scratch sides. The starting catcher was Hank and he went on one side, with his back-up, the Chinese boy called Ray Chong, on the other team. Merle was starting pitcher and he took John on his team. To the English boy's surprise, the second-string pitcher was Krysty King.

While everyone was getting sorted out, the girl showed John around the baseball diamond, pointing out the boundaries of the field. There were some rather dusty trees on two sides, but immediately in front of the batter's plate John could make out the sun glinting on windows of some kind. It looked around a hundred yards or so away. Just about within range of a very long and hard-hit homer.

'What's that?' he asked.

'What?'

'There. The sun's flashin' off some glass or windows or something.'

'Oh, that's Ted's greenhouse.'

'What on earth's that? And who's Ted when he's at home?'

The English phrase threw Krysty for a moment. 'Oh, I get it. Hey, Merle, you know the story about Ted Williams and that old greenhouse yonder. Tell John 'bout it.'

The tall boy wandered up, wearing cut-off shorts and a torn T-shirt. His long hair was tied back in a pony-tail with a length of baling twine.

'Ted's broken glass, huh? You goin' to try for it, my man?'

'I don't know what it is.'

'Sure. Now, I heard this story from my old man and there's a load of other guys here heard it the same way. But that doesn't mean it's true. All I know is that every kid in this part of San Diego's been trying for years, including me, to hit a straight home run out over that fence and break a pane of glass in the old greenhouse there.'

'How does Ted Williams come . . . ? Oh, I get it. He came from the city, right? And the story is that when he was playing here as a kid, he did it. Broke the window. And then he went on to become one of the all-time greats. That it?'

Merle nodded. 'That's it, John. I heard some guy in the early seventies did it and went on to play for the Phillies, but I'm not so sure.'

'How far is it?' asked John, shading his eyes with his hand.

'Too far!' laughed Krysty. 'Come on, John. Let's go play ball.'

Merle asked John if he wanted to go to second base, which is one of the easier fielding positions. Taking a deep breath, he said he wanted to play short-stop if that was OK with Merle.

'Sure, John. If *you're* sure? It's a pretty tough position to play. Specially for someone who maybe doesn't know the game that well.'

'Like to try.'

'For sure.'

John saw that Hank, also a left-handed player, was going to be first at the bat, so he positioned himself between first and second bases. Merle struck Hank out, to the black boy's disgust, bringing up another boy, whose name John didn't know. He was a right-handed hitter and John moved accordingly, shifting between second and third.

Merle saw him and came jogging over. 'Nice one, man. Good thinking. You *do* know a bit about playing ball.'

The batter plopped one up in the air, over the heads of the infielders and reached first. The next boy also singled, bringing runners on first and second. The fourth person at bat was one of the girls. She was a very tall black girl with plaited hair. John noticed she had incredibly long finger-nails on her left hand.

She hit the second pitch from Merle like a rocket towards John, the ball bobbling in the ruts of the field. But he kept his eye on it, concentrating hard, and in one easy motion scooped it up into his new glove, transferred it to his left hand, and threw the girl out before she could reach first base.

'Back here!' shouted John, beckoning the first baseman to throw the ball back to him. He caught it neatly and tagged the boy running to third.

Two out in one play and a round of cheers and applause for John's quickness.

As the beginner, John was put last in the batting order for his side. First inning was completed without him getting a chance at the bat, thanks to some excellent dipping curve pitches from Krysty King.

He was disappointed not to get to the plate, know-

119

ing that it would have helped his nerves. But he continued to do well in the field.

In the second inning he caught a cloud-scraping pop-up ball and also managed to throw one of the runners out as he tried to slide into the base.

The next inning began with a series of single hits and a walk, putting players on first, second and third bases. John came to bat in that position, knowing it was called 'having the bases loaded'. If he was to fulfil a dream and hit a homer, then all four batters would score a run. A grand-slam homer.

The sun was still glinting off the glass roof and walls of Ted William's legendary greenhouse in the distance. The other runners were all looking in his direction. Merle from third, a girl from second and Ray Chong from first. All waiting to see what he'd do.

'Good luck, John,' muttered Hank from behind the catcher's mask.

Krysty winked at him from the pitcher's mound, winding up and throwing. John struck too fast at it, missing it early.

'Strike one,' said the boy umpiring.

The sun was very bright, bouncing off the distant glass. John wiped sweat off his forehead and got ready for the second pitch.

Krysty threw him a late curve. In his anxiety John held back; finally seeing it was going to be a strike when it was too late. His swing was painfully slow and hesitant.

Amongst the boys and girls sitting on the cropped turf, watching him, John was sure he heard someone mention the name of Eugene.

'Strike two.'

Hank Wexner took off his catcher's face-mask and straightened up. Clearing his throat and spitting in the dust, he said 'You gotta relax, John. You're tighter than a coiled rattler. You got a good natural swing there, but it's all going wrong. Slow it down and relax. Now go to it. Play ball, man.'

'Thanks,' muttered John, shuffling his trainers to make sure his feet didn't slip when he swung. Krysty was sitting back on her haunches on the mound, watching him. Looking for a sign from the catcher what kind of pitch to try. Nodding as she saw the finger-signal.

Merle gave John a clenched-fist gesture of grinning encouragement.

He thought of his life in England and of Rick Okie and of how it had felt when he'd swung and hit the sweet spot. John braced himself, bat almost touching the back of his head, wrists cocked and ready.

Krysty let the pitch go, fast and straight. John watched it all the way, uncoiling his swing and feeling the wonderful, soft jarring shudder as he connected.

He didn't bother to start running, knowing that the baseball was going to fly for a very long way, straight and true. It drilled down through the middle of the field, high over the heads of everyone.

John kept his eyes on it, mouth half-open, unable to mask his delight.

'Hey, it's gonna . . .' began Hank Wexner, his voice fading away in awe.

The ball drove on and on, not seeming to lose any of its height or speed.

On and on.

At the last moment, in the stunned silence, John closed his eyes, hearing the faint but unmistakable tinkling sound of broken glass.

'Lift-off,' he said.